You're in Game!

LitRPG stories
from bestselling authors

Vasily Mahanenko
Andrei Livadny
Michael Atamanov
Andrew Novak
Pavel Kornev
Alexey Osadchuk

Magic Dome Books

TABLE OF CONTENTS:

P. KORNEV. COUNTDOWN.............................. 1

V. MAHANENKO. SHAMANIC RITES................. 47

A. LIVADNY. PURGATORY.................................. 67

M. ATAMANOV. THRONE WORLD.................... 103

A. NOVAK. THE BEST QUEST........................... 145

A. OSADCHUK. THE DATE............................... 185

V. MAHANENKO. THE STORY OF A RAID......... 219

COUNTDOWN

A LITRPG SHORT STORY

BY PAVEL KORNEV

G ADGETS are evil.

My silenced smartphone vibrated in my breast pocket just as I was trying to whip out the gun. I loosed off two slugs in rapid succession. Still, I didn't even need to check the target. I knew I'd missed.

Having holstered my 911, I unhurriedly reached into my denim shirt pocket for the still-vibrating phone. I glanced at the screen and cussed.

Did I say gadgets were evil? Oh no. They're evil's henchmen.

The real Inferno-class evil is when your employer calls you on your day off. Somehow I doubted he wanted to invite me to a barbecue party at his place. Quite the opposite, more likely.

Still hoping that it might be about some stupid formality which wouldn't disrupt my scheduled hundred-shot practice, I pulled off the earmuffs and swiped the screen, accepting the call.

"Code red," the familiar voice said. "The file is in your inbox."

Code red? Did we even have one?

I was about to ask him as much but stopped myself just in time. "I'm opening it," I said.

Before leaving the yard and going back

indoors, I did check the targets though. Surprisingly enough, one of the two slugs had hit the "corpse" printout straight in the forehead. Still, I wasn't in the mood to celebrate the fact. Not anymore.

I PULLED the plastic cover off the game capsule. I hadn't been planning on logging in today. Still, I booted up and lay on its comfortable bed which looked a bit like those used by dentists, with foam rollers massaging your body under the soft upholstery.

Immediately I half-rose again and removed the holster from my belt. I decided against locking the gun away. Instead I just left it lying on the rotating side table next to the keyboard and the monitor.

The icon of an unread message blinked in the corner of the screen. Disappointingly, it turned out to be only a promotional letter advertising the new *Be Yourself!* project. For those gamers fed up with seven-foot Barbarians and DD-size Amazons, the game designers offered to have their own bodies scanned, then level them up — or rather, level up their 3D models, anatomically correct in every detail.

Personally, I'd chosen that option already at the beta testing stage. In the past, I used to play all sorts: from burly knights to nimble rogues and Elven archers, and every time it had taken me ages to get used to a new body.

The game console finished booting and played a soft jingle. I slid on the wire-free VR helmet. Before activating it though, I refreshed my inbox, discovered a new message and opened the attachment. It contained all the instructions, coordinates and access codes I might need.

For a brief moment, everything went dark. Then I found myself in my Dashboard. Its design was deliberately Spartan: the players' minds needed time to adjust to their new environment.

Ghostlike, I slid past the row of the choicest level-99 characters: the highest level currently possible. A kilt-clad Barbarian with a two-handed sword; an Elf with a longbow; a King's rifleman with a musket and a saber; a pirate Orc armed with a cutlass and two pistols under his belt, and lots of others. They differed only in skin color: each and every one of them was me, allowing me to settle into any of them in no time.

Still, I habitually chose my favorite char: the Dark Wanderer, his eyes glowing crimson with infernal flames. A warlock assassin was a perfect fit for today's job.

Ignoring the numerous maintenance screens displaying his stats and skill/ability branches, I reached for a shimmering envelope-shaped icon: a message from the technical department. Immediately the long sequence of nines in my XP column was replaced by the infinity sign.

A new status appeared: *Demi-God,* opening a new ability branch. Its name was *Divine Magic.*

Oh, well. The game developers had every right to consider themselves the new demiurges: creators of a new world and a new reality.

Then I was thrust into that world upwards, like a corpse forced out of a freshly dug grave.

The next moment I stood amid a forest glade overgrown with tall grass. Insects buzzed in the air; at a distance, a woodpecker picked at a tree. The air, fresh and pure, was heavy with strange floral scents.

I took a few deep breaths and laughed, drunk with my new almighty power. Even though the code I'd received in the mail hadn't contained the key to true immortality like the fabled "IDDQD" of old, it had improved my already maxed-out skills and abilities manifold.

+50% bonus to every stat I had, +100% to all damage dealt by cold steel and +300% to protection from magic spells. Add to this non-stop mana restoration, and my Dark Wanderer became a true killing machine.

Billowing shadows swirled around me. The grass at my feet withered. I had to take control of my new power and conceal it within me. Run-of-the-mill sorcerers may have had access to higher-level spells — but Dark Wanderers knew how to hide their aura, keeping their abilities under wraps until the last possible moment. The last for our victims, that is.

My mind seemed to have split, allowing me to see myself as if through another person's eyes.

A gaunt dark-haired man stood in a circle of withered grass. He wore a gray cloak over his dark green jerkin. A broadsword and a dagger hung heavily from his wide leather belt. His left hand glittered with magic rings, each more powerful than the next. The relic ring containing the Fire of Holy Exorcism had cost me so dearly in that wretched bone-shattering quest that I'd kept it more as a souvenir than for anything else.

Personal and gear stats began flickering on the screens, reporting the items' remaining Durability. Once the data was saved and synchronized, the split personality effect was gone too.

Powerful wings rent the air. A huge raven landed onto my shoulder. His claws sank into my skin, hurting even through the thick cloth.

"Direction north east," he croaked. "You're expected. Go!"

Having delivered his message, Munin the Raven — the in-game automatic communication module — shot back up into the air and disappeared into the heavens.

I began walking directly through the woods in the direction he'd pointed. My high leather boots protected my legs from the dew. Soon I discovered a trail threading amid the oaks.

A blurred outline flashed past nearby bushes. In the forest, Elves could be a real pain in the butt. Knowing that, I activated Divine Vision. The spell revealed the glowing of several auras belonging to players scattered throughout the trees. They were definitely players — not NPCs. Unlike the True Vision available to sorcerers, my professional spells allowed me to tell the difference.

All the Elves were level 99, their stats hidden.

Definitely not players. Maintenance experts, more likely. *Code red*, whatever that was supposed to mean.

"Keep on going," the raven croaked. "You're expected!"

The Elves hadn't even looked at me. The path soon took me to a muddy road. I followed it until I came to the enormous dome of the Diamond Veil. The security perimeter had been reinforced with restricted-access Divine Magic, its Durability stat window left blank.

And on top of it all, they had a Higher

Paladin of the Crimson Sun Order posted next to four Elementals summoned from the Plane of Fire.

Tongues of colorless flames licked his ruby-tinted armor. I was dying to give him a good whack with the darkest combat spell I had. Still, I overcame my char's urge. Yes, you heard right. As a player levels up, his virtual body soaks up his actions and decisions, transforming his most repeated behavioral patterns into instincts. The higher a player's level, the bigger this transformation is.

A nice warlock? Do me a favor.

Under his watchful glare, I approached the Diamond Veil and pressed my hand to it, feeling the cold of a hostile magic.

"Go!" Munin the Raven croaked again.

Bracing myself, I stepped through the sparkling mist toward the ranger's hut it concealed.

The hut's back yard was crowded with golems rambling about. There was no sign of their alchemist controller anywhere. The bots were in autonomous mode, busy studying severed limbs scattered on the blood-soaked earth.

I counted the remains of five human bodies. Their simple jerkins revealed mithril chainmail underneath, its links ripped by inhuman blows. The place was littered with fragments of charmed swords and broken muskets.

I selected all the bodies, opened their stats and chuckled in surprise. The dead men had been anything but newbs.

Class: forest rangers
Levels: 43 to 52

They'd had plenty of specialization bonuses and magic artifacts. Judging by the nature of their wounds, they had come across some creature of Inferno. In which case I had no idea why they'd had to ask me to come. A demon against five top-level rangers was a fair enough ratio. The guys had been down on their luck, that was all.

But the moment I entered the ranger's hut, it all became clear.

Blood was the first thing I noticed. The floorboards were completely drenched in it, to the point where the gutted body of the sixth victim failed to produce any effect. I tried to focus on it but its stat window was completely empty.

"A player?" I asked a puny old alchemist perched on a stool.

The old man pried himself from his notebook, raised his orange glasses to his forehead and nodded.

"What's the urgency?" I asked, studying the skinned body.

"He got stuck," the old man explained. "Or she, rather. It's a girl. Sixteen years old."

I felt queasy. Not because of the stench of blood. Not at all.

This is full immersion gameplay, you see. Here, virtual reality deceives all your senses, making pain just as acute as it is in real life. But there's still a certain threshold where defenses kick in. When this happens, you first watch your char writhe in agony, then you're thrown back into the main menu where you cry again — not with pain this time but with all the XP you've just lost. But if you're stuck in the game while someone skins you alive... the pain is such you can just go nuts on the spot.

"What could have caused it?" I asked.

"We're looking into it," he pointed at the body. "Your job is to find the guy who did it."

"What do you mean, find? Can't you just check the logs?"

The alchemist removed his glasses and began wiping them with a scrap of cloth. He'd posed his feet on the stool's crossbar in order not to soil his pointy leather shoes with blood.

"So what's with the logs?" I nudged him.

"A glitch in the Frankfurt data center..." he

began, pointing his glasses at me. "No, it's not that! It's none of your business, anyway! Just find the murderer and set a pack of Hell Hounds on him. Hurry! The sooner we retrieve the... the *trophies*, the sooner we can get her out of her coma."

"So that's what it is, then? That's what *Be Yourself!* is about? This is a digital imprint of her own body, isn't it? Is that why it glitched? Because it got dismantled?"

"We're looking into it," the alchemist insisted. "Just do your job, will you? The murderer used an astral portal. He's playing as a Demonic Metamorph. That's all we know about him at the moment."

"Tracking him down isn't going to be easy."

"That's exactly why we hired *you* to do the job!"

Oh was it? Somehow I didn't think so.

The reason they'd hired me was because I wasn't on their payroll. I was a freelancer — an outsider.

Formally, the murderer hadn't broken any of the game's rules. The PvP mode was one of its main attractions. Naturally, the admins didn't want such incidents to become public. But that didn't mean they were prepared to suffer problem players gladly. All those top-level perverts, serial killers and stalkers on the prowl for virtual and real-life celebrities was bad for business. That's when they turned to people like me.

You could call us scalp hunters, I suppose.

It's very easy to make a player's virtual life unbearable, repeatedly killing them, stripping them of XP or robbing them clean of their hard-earned artifacts. I'm a stalker, too. The difference is, I only stalk very, very bad guys. I mean, *really* bad — bad even by the game's all-permissive standards.

"Get on with it!" the alchemist snapped.

I laid my hand on the sticky floor, then drew a wide vertical circle in the air. A bloody ring hovered above the floor. The spell sliced through the in-game reality, opening a portal into the astral plane. It exuded a spine-chilling cold.

Calmly I stepped through the portal into a boundless void. The only things disrupting its infinity were the fine threads of power lines and wisps of digital reality drifting through empty space.

The void latched onto me with hundreds of invisible tentacles, greedily sucking me dry of my mana. Still, my access to Divine Magic made my resources practically limitless. Unhurriedly I recited the search spell, binding the victim's blood on my hand to her skin the murderer had taken away as a *trophy*.

The scarlet droplets covering my fingers

began to boil and form the finest red cord reaching out into the distance. I hurried to clutch at it. The next moment I was jerked out of my place and pulled across the void fast and sharp as if I were a bolt released from a crossbow.

The astral plane whizzed past me like a gray shadow as the blood magic pulled me after the murderer. That was a mistake. The barely noticeable dot in front of me zoomed into a large inky spot which grew a great many ghostly tentacles. They reached out toward me, impatient to catch me and take me in.

I barely had enough time to fling the Spear of Shadows.

In the brief moment of my travel through the astral plane, the combat spell had weakened 48%. This was the reason why, instead of ripping the phantom guard apart and scattering his fragments in space, he had only been torn in two. One of his tentacles lashed against my leg, breaking the blood line. I was thrown aside and swept away by a whirlwind. The spawn of the Dark was level 30: the highest possible for creatures of Inferno. Now it split into two level-10 creatures which attacked me with a renewed vigor. Still, my promptly cast magic sphere protected me from their first attack, buying me enough time to draw the portal formula back into the real world.

Immediately a box popped up, counting down the spell's dwindling Durability. I dashed for the portal which had just begun to open when something grabbed my left ankle and pulled me back, strongly and unhesitantly.

Critical damage received: dislocated foot!

Overcoming the power of the pull, I grabbed at the wilting grass and strained my every muscle, forcing myself through the gaping split between the two realities. The phantom tentacle reached for me through the opening — but, assaulted by the sun's rays, began to twitch, smoking. I slashed it with my Elven dagger cast with a special spell which turned out to be 2 pt. more than the creature's immunity to cold steel.

The dagger cut clean through the tentacle entwining my foot and crumbled it to dust.

"Dammit!" I hurried to scramble away from the closing portal.

The attack of the guardian spirit had thrown me off course. Finding the murderer wasn't going to be as easy now as I'd originally planned.

Still, somehow I didn't think the error was that big. My target must be around somewhere.

I limped down a small lane, feeling for a

healing potion in my pocket. I gulped it down and hurried on, free from the distracting pain.

Health: +7/1500
Critical damage neutralized
The agility penalty removed
Stamina restored

The lane brought me out into the back yard of some tavern or other. I turned a corner and found myself in a large square packed with humans, Elves, orcs and all sorts of unidentifiable creatures. Music played; revelers poured their cups from the kegs set on the pavement.

My Divine Vision couldn't help me much here. My eyes watered with all the countless name tags hovering over the players' heads.

Oh no! This was probably some kind of event. Just my luck!

Wings flapped overhead. Munin the Raven landed on my shoulder.

"Suspicious activity in the victim's account detected," he croaked. "Someone posing as her has invited a player known as Alex999 to meet her in the Rusty Axe Inn."

"Posing as her?" I repeated, casting wary glances around me. "How sure are you it's not her?"

"The victim's consciousness is trapped in her dead body. It can't be her."

"Are you implying that someone has hacked into her account?"

"It's highly probable."

I noticed a shop sign sporting a hefty two-handed battle axe and hurried toward it, skirting the square in the direction of a well-built stone house and doing my best not to push and shove my way through the crowd too hard. Soon I slowed down, however. "How fast you think you can block the hacker?"

"We're working on it. Still, the server is in overload because of this event. We can't just unplug the whole cluster. We need to pinpoint his exact location first-"

Suddenly the raven's voice changed. Now he sounded like the alchemist I'd left in the forest hut. "Critical error! The game has been breached! The victim has been made comatose on purpose! Stop him! Stop him now!"

"Stop whom?" I asked.

"Alex999 shouldn't meet with the metamorph! Alex999 is the nickname of Alexander Reiss, Jr.! The son of-"

Yes, yes. The son of Alexander Reiss Sr., our billionaire investor.

"I want you to listen closely," the alchemist hurried, using the raven as a communications channel. "We've managed to recover some of the logs. The metamorph didn't just steal the dead girl's identity. He used the server's breach to block her mind in the game and gain access to her account. The victim is a personal friend of Reiss, Jr. Answering her invitation, he logged in unaccompanied by his bodyguards, using the digital copy of his own body. The hacker is after him, not her! Our guys are still busy fixing the hole in the code. You must make sure they don't meet!"

"I'll see what I can do."

"Just do it! Please! Don't you understand what's at stake?"

Oh yes I did. An accident with the billionaire brat might mean closing the game down. If the hacker managed to render *him* comatose, our rankings would sink faster than you could say *Titanic*. Also, I'd lose my job.

Which wasn't a nice prospect, I had to admit.

I shoved the inn door open and stepped inside. Much to my disappointment, no one in its large room looked remotely like a billionaire brat.

Two drunks by the bar were busy getting sloshed on cheap brandy under a fat innkeeper's disapproving glare. A lanky waiter was half-heartedly dragging a mop across the greasy floor. A table by the door was taken by an Elf and a young girl, her breast disproportionately large for her slender frame.

My gaze alighted on the latter. Not to stare at her erect nipples showing through her blouse, no: I was busy opening her and her friend's stats windows. The Elf turned out to be a level 39 Forest Dancer and his girlfriend, a level 27 Marsh Witch.

The innkeeper turned to the sound of the front door slamming shut behind me. He yawned and covered his mouth with his meaty hand. "All the rooms are taken."

I nodded my understanding and headed for the bar. "No chance of a hot meal?"

Admittedly, food didn't interest me in the slightest. I sensed the presence of the blood cord linking me to the murderer. He was here somewhere. Upstairs, most likely.

"Some chow, you mean?" the innkeeper sounded confused. He bent down and looked under the bar. "Yeah, I suppose so..."

Elves are a noiseless lot, you have to give them that. I would never have known he'd stolen up on me had it not been for his clumsy girlfriend. One of her heels clanked on the floor as she scrambled down her high stool. The Elf lunged onto me, whipping out a curved dagger from its sheath. One of the drunks swung round and hurled a half-empty brandy bottle at me.

Shadow Mode: On
+50% to Speed and Reaction Times
+25% to Accuracy and Damage
+20% to your chance of dealing critical damage
Duration: 20 sec

Color drained from the scene, clouding it in a gray haze. Sounds subsided. Like an off-white lightning, I swung in place and leaped toward the Elf, dodging his blow. The dagger whizzed over my head: my Dodge was 30% better than his Accuracy with all its bonuses and perks taken together. I reverse-gripped my knife, slicing the enemy's leg directly across the ligament and sending Mr. Pointy Ears tumbling across the floor.

A red-lettered warning added to the battle logs, reporting a critical penalty to the Elf's Agility due to the damaged ligament and another -10 pt./sec Health caused by damage to his popliteal vein.

Without stopping, I lunged for the witch who was busy growing a magic lightning bolt between her hands, and stabbed her in the neck.

Another red line added to the logs. My knife had sliced through the artery, letting out a thick stream of blood. I swung round to meet the "drunks" who were about to attack me from behind. I kicked a stool from under the first one's feet, grabbed the second one's cudgel arm and buried my knife under his armpit, just above the edge of his sleeveless chainmail shirt.

The blow proved lethal. The man tumbled to the floor, his Life bar colorless. His partner jumped back to his feet, forcing me to slash him across his eyes.

The Shadow Mode's +20% to critical damage kicked in again, blinding the guy. A new symbol appeared over his head: an eye crossed with a red line.

By then, the wounded Elf had already reached for the dagger he'd dropped in his fall. I pressed my knee against his back. The slim blade of my knife slid easily into the space between his spine and the base of his skull. His Life bar reset to zero. The Elf stopped moving.

A crossbow snapped. I twisted my body, feinting my cloak like a bullfighter. Oozing magic, the crossbow bolt passed uselessly through the fabric and pierced the wall's wooden paneling. The wood split and turned black, billowing smoke.

This time my Dodge was only 1 pt. higher than the crossbow attack's Accuracy. So when the innkeeper bent down to reload his light crossbow, I unhesitantly threw my knife at him. My advanced throwing weapon skill in combination with Shadow Mode sent the knife exactly where I aimed it, burying the blade in the innkeeper's eye socket.

With the Shadow Mode already expiring, I finished off the blinded drunkard.

My head swam. The gray haze receded. The pale blood staining the whole place turned bright red again. Sounds returned, loud and clear.

Shadow Mode: Off
-15% penalty to Strength and Stamina
-10% penalty to Speed, Accuracy and Reaction Times
-5% penalty to Damage
-25% to your chance to deal critical damage

The penalty expires in: 15 min

I heard a pattering sound. Someone was clapping their hands.

The lanky waiter.

"Not bad," he laughed, then gave his mop a mighty kick, breaking the handle off and twirling it in front of him like a proper Staff Master, turning a humble mop handle into a whooshing, ghostly disk.

Although he'd blocked his personal data, my Divine Vision forced his stats tab to open.

Main Class: Spear Bearer
Secondary class: Telekinesis Mage
Specialization: Puppeteer
Level, 83
Health, 1256/1256
Status, co-chairman of the Free Lancers clan
Name: Marius Thorne

Someone else might find this mercenary hard to tackle, but not me. Still, I had my work cut out for me here — simply because I had to use combat spells with caution for fear of alerting the murderer.

I glanced at the Shadow Mode cooldown timer and winced. I still had another 14.5 minutes until it was live again, and two more hours until the next teleport.

What a cunning bastard!

Munin the Raven sprang onto my shoulder from a ceiling beam. "You must pull Alexander out of the game!" he croaked. "You should kill his char, if necessary!"

"Why can't you just unplug him?"

"His capsule is blocked! If we unplug him, he might suffer brain damage!"

A girl appeared at the top of the stairs. She was slim and pretty, with bloodshot eyes and faint traces of cuts on her pale skin. She was supporting a young guy, leading him downstairs. The guy had the vacant stare of a stoned junkie.

Even my Divine Vision failed to open his personal information. It wasn't really blocked: it was as if it didn't exist!

Wretched hacker!

"Alex!" I shouted but the kid staggered on, his body limp as if sleepwalking. The mercenary headed for me, still swinging his stick.

I didn't need to stay quiet any longer. I thrust my left hand forward, growling with pain as a clot of ashen-gray shadows escaped my fingertips. The combat spell broke the enemy's stick and hit him in the chest. His immunity to magic failed. The damage was twice his current health reading. The "spear bearer" exploded with a nasty popping sound, sending cascades of blood, flesh and bone fragments all over the inn.

I dipped my right hand into a pool of blood and shook it, willing the scarlet droplets to freeze in mid-air, then used them to draw the summoning formula for Hell Hounds. They were just another type of service bots, not exactly sentient but fast and invulnerable.

My actions made the girl stop. She was surrounded by a digital aura that didn't belong to her. Apparently, her appearance wasn't the only thing the metamorph murderer had borrowed.

"Wrong timing," the creature waved an annoyed hand in the air, showering me with lightning.

The furniture unlucky enough to be in its wake turned to ash. Me, I didn't even try to dodge it. I just threw my left hand in the air and made a simple figure with my fingers, summoning the Veil of Darkness from a quick access slot.

This top-level defense magic had no problem absorbing my enemy's attack. The lightning didn't touch me. The raven, however, disintegrated in a shower of binary code. My shoulder smarted where his claws had clutched.

You've received Damage!
Health: -15/1485

For a brief moment, my head swam. The kidnapper didn't linger. He grabbed the kid and dragged him downstairs into the cellar.

Grinding my teeth with the still-painful itch in my shoulder, I resumed the summoning ritual. Or should I say, I attempted to do so.

The droplets of blood in the air had turned gray and become unresponsive to my will. I tried to repeat the formula but it was inactive. And not just that! My entire Divine Magic tab was blocked as if the raven's death had canceled my access.

"Shit!" I hurried after them, taking the

stairs down three at a time. A bricked-up doorway rose before me.

Unhesitantly I used the Magic Ram. The spell destroyed the obstacle with habitual ease. I stepped through the cloud of dust into the cellar. A summoning formula was hastily drawn on the floor, the room's dark corners crawling with dreadful shadows. Cold breathed in my face. Frost was rapidly covering the walls and floor with its silvery swirls. I felt tired and desperate.

Mental attack: 68
Immunity to powers of Inferno: 33
Immunity to hypnosis magic: 25
Class bonus: 12
Level bonus: 10
Attack has failed

I forced myself to overcome the spirits' mental attack, then shouted the Holy Exorcism formula. The words of the spell rolled over the cellar like a wall of fire, burning the summoned minions of the Dark whose inferior level hadn't withstood the blow from Higher Magic.

My shoulder smarted again.

I tugged at my collar, pulling it aside to check on the claw marks. They were infected and surrounded by the black script of unknown codes. Something alien had penetrated my body and it didn't look good.

I didn't care.

I ran the whole length of the cellar stacked with beer kegs and bundles of sausages hanging off the ceiling. I was about to kick open the grate at its far end when I noticed the haze of protective charms surrounding it. So I decided to teleport instead.

My head swam in a bout of nausea. A translucent maintenance message appeared before my eyes,

Your current level doesn't allow access to the requested spell. It has been temporarily removed from your skill tree.

"Excuse me?" I shouted. "What the f-"

My Dark Wanderer was the highest level possible. It just couldn't happen!

Then I realized, horrified, that my XP was dropping rapidly — nullifying all my skills and spells!

My personal stat window now read,

Status, Dark Wanderer
Level, 68

Roaring with rage, I used the primitive — but no less effective — Fist of Fury to bash the wall next to the grate. There! And again!

Mana: — 50/950
Mana: — 50/900

My magic powers began to dwindle. Still, the wall succumbed to my fifth blow, collapsing and bringing the grate down. I jumped into the opening — and ducked, rolling over the floor to avoid the jet of magic flames coming from a rune mounted on the wall. My 30% immunity to fire allowed me to avoid serious injury but I was forced to pull off and discard my burning cloak.

A stone staircase loomed through the haze. I ran toward it, hearing measured footsteps coming down. A Steel Knight descended toward me. Luckily, his flamberge sword proved too long. Its undulating blade grazed the low ceiling, allowing me to leap closer and attack him with Elven Rust. The spell worked like a dream, turning the golem's armor into a rusted pile of junk metal. Its durability dropped 95%. Assisted by Bone Crusher, my fist punched right through it, my arm sinking elbow deep into the Knight's flesh.

I received an almighty blow on my back from the sword's hilt. My ribs cracked. My breathing seized. Still, I kept my footing and ripped the Knight's heart out of his chest. It dissolved into a nasty reactive chemical in my hand. The golem's orange Life bar turned gray. It collapsed in a heap of lifeless armor.

Health: -150/1335
You've received critical damage to your chest!
-10% penalty to Stamina, Agility and Reaction Times
-20% penalty to damage dealt by two-handed slashing weapons

I stepped over the rusty heap and walked up the stairs, sifting through whatever spells were still available. First, I activated True Vision in order to locate the guards the metamorph had posted outside. Then I activated the Haze of Invisibility and ran out into the inn's back yard.

I was met by a line of golem crossbowmen facing the door. They loosed off their bolts at me — but a promptly cast Magic Wind blew the heavy projectiles out of my path.

Attack Intensity: 100x5
Defense: 750
Attack has failed

I responded by casting Diamond Sickle. The spell turned out to be surprisingly weak, only downing three of the four golems, the last one in the row only sliced halfway through.

I was forced to attack the crossbowman with a trivial fireball. The blow threw him onto his back without dealing any damage at all. The golem wriggled on the ground, trying to scramble back to his feet. I grabbed the first thing my hand chanced on — a sledgehammer — and brought it down onto his enclosed helmet, again and again, until gearwheels from his pulverized head went flying all over the yard.

An unbearable fatigue came over me. I dropped the suddenly too heavy sledgehammer and gulped a healing potion.

Heath, +165/700
Critical damage removed
Penalties canceled

My head cleared somewhat. The pain in my back subsided. I pulled the shirt off my inflamed shoulder. The mysterious symbols kept spreading over my skin.

My XP continued to dwindle, rapidly approaching zero. And with it, all the months I'd spent in the game were going down the drain.

My stat window now read,
Status, Dark Wanderer
Level, 44

"I'll kill the bastard!" I growled, knowing perfectly well I couldn't kill him anymore.

None of the higher magic was available to me now. I could only use the most primitive of spells. My weapon skills — both firearms and cold steel — began to deteriorate, too. One by one, my abilities and skills turned gray and unresponsive, then disappeared.

Nevertheless, blood magic kept connecting me to the metamorph murderer. Which meant I could still bring the technical support experts to him. With the raven's death I couldn't contact them directly but every town here had post offices — the nearest one located right here in the city square.

I hurried there, panting. By the time I reached it, I was seriously out of breath — something that hadn't happened to me since my first days in the game.

I checked my stats again. My level had dropped to 35. Even the expiration of the fifteen-minute Shadow Mode penalty failed to cheer me up.

THE POST OFFICE was empty. The postmaster sat in his cubicle, looking utterly bored. The duty wizard was busy polishing his crystal ball with a cloth. A burly guard sat by the open window, munching peanuts.

"How can I help you?" the postmaster flashed me a professional smile, ignoring my disheveled appearance.

"I need to see the sorcerer," I told him as I walked past his cubicle, pointing at the crystal ball. "May I?"

With a good-humored smile, the post wizard moved away from his communications artifact. But the moment my hand lay on the cold smooth crystal, his smile evaporated.

A warning flashed in my mental view,

Your social status has been changed!
Your social status has been changed!
Your social status has been changed!

From now on, you're a stranger!
You're an outcast!
An enemy!

I was an enemy! Every player's rightful prey and target! This was the system's way of marking cheaters and the most incorrigible PKs. But me?

I didn't get the chance to answer my own question. The sorcerer's eyes flashed with a crimson fire. I dealt him a lethal chopping blow, burying his nose in his skull and resetting his Life bar to zero.

Immediately I swung round, lashed out

with a knife at the guard who'd finally left his position by the window, then hurried after the post master busy disappearing through the back door. I caught up with him and slammed his back with my hand, pounding him face into the wall.

The post master went belly first onto the stonework, then slid to the ground. A translucent icon appeared over his head, reporting his Unconscious status.

I heard suppressed wheezing behind my back. Steel rustled against leather.

Attack: 45
Dodge: 59
Attack has failed

I ducked to one side. The guard missed me, burying his sword into one of the desks instead. He was pressing his other hand to his slashed neck: the wound hadn't been lethal after all. Bug-eyed with fury, he lunged at me again. This time I didn't attempt to dodge his attack; instead, I parried it with a heavy stool, then gave him a good whack on the head with it.

The guy dropped where he stood. I straddled him and stabbed his face, aiming for his eye, but missed and sliced through his temple instead. I stabbed him again, going for his neck this time.

The guard wriggled, trying to shake me off, but I kept stabbing, the knife handle in my fingers slippery with blood. It took me a lot of fumbling and fighting to finally finish him off.

I rose to my feet, covered in blood, and took a peek out of the window. One look was enough to know they wouldn't let me out of the city alive. The Enemy status was worse than a brand mark: every newb would feel obliged to hurl a fireball at me or take a musket shot at my back.

Not so long ago, I could have stealthed up and left this place unnoticed, lurking in the shadows. But not now. Defeating the guard hadn't brought me any XP which kept dwindling rapidly; and with it, my combat skills disappeared one by one. In the meantime, the mysterious symbols kept spreading over my body, creeping from under my jacket sleeves onto my hands and wrists.

Status, Wanderer
Level, 29

I glanced at the body at my feet, pressed my hand to the dead guard's chest and used one of the few remaining Illusion spells. The corpse self-immolated, turning into a charred skeleton. I nearly crumbled under the half-ton weight of the

Second Skin spell popular with newb sorcerers and necromancers. The last of my mana began disappearing fast.

Mana consumption: -1/sec

Resisting fatigue, I left the post office and hurried out of town, hoping to clear its limits before the spell drained me of the last of my magic.

I didn't make it. A bout of pain surged through me as I stole along a quiet side street. My borrowed guise quivered, dissolving into nothing. That wouldn't have been so bad but just ahead of me I could see a tavern and two identical-looking musketeers standing by the hitching post.

Both were level 22 against my 20. I wasn't a Dark Wanderer any longer but a regular one. My magic abilities opened at level 21.

My teeth ached with a bad premonition. Still, I kept walking, ignoring the suspiciously dark shadow enveloping its tall plank fence.

I didn't need True Vision to identify a magic illusion. I was an expert at these kinds of things.

"Do you need help?" one of the musketeers moved toward me. He was a mere twenty feet away from me.

By then, I'd already come near the

suspicious shadow.

"Let me through," I said.

"But-"

I whipped out the broadsword and slashed at the illusion, burying the blade deep inside. Blood gushed onto the road, mixing with the dust. A young sorceress materialized from the shadows and dropped into the gutter, her collar bone bleeding. The nearest musketeer hurried to raise his flint pistol.

I got to him first. A charmed diamond flashed in the ring on my left pinkie, releasing a fireball. It momentarily struggled, caught in the man's protective aura, then overcame its resistance and exploded in his face.

> **Fireball (a single-use artifact): 444**
> **Shield of Odin: 399**
> **Defense has failed**
> **Damage: -45/355**
> **Additional effect: Stun/Blindness.**
> **Duration: 30 sec**

The guy pressed his hands to his eye, spinning in place. Another musket clapped from the direction of the hitching post. The heavy ball kicked me in the chest, pushing me onto my back. Luckily, my Skin of Rock ability was still active. I got away with a few broken ribs.

Damage: -125

Skin of Rock: Damage absorption, +125

Additional damage: critical damage to your ribs

-45% penalty to Stamina, Agility and Reaction Times

-50% penalty to damage dealt by two-handed slashing weapons

I tried to breathe but couldn't. My chest was on fire. My head was bursting. I was obliged to use my last remaining healing potion.

I gulped the bitter drink and rolled over to one side, placing the wounded musketeer between me and his partner.

"John, move aside!" the second musketeer shouted, reaching for a flint pistol from his saddle holster.

His wounded partner didn't seem to hear him. He must have been delirious with pain. This game was for real.

Brandishing his pistol, the second musketeer dashed toward his friend. I was quicker though. I whipped out a pistol from behind the wounded guy's belt and shot his partner in the head. The heavy lead slug caused a critical hit, rending his skull apart. I changed my grip on the gun, stepped back and pistol-whipped John, smashing his temple.

The guy dropped face down, sporting the Unconsciousness icon. His Health bar began to dwindle rapidly due to an internal bleeding.

I threw the discharged pistol into the ditch, picked up the musket lying in the roadside dust and hurried toward the hitching post. I untethered the horse closest to me, climbed into the saddle and urged it hard, trying to put as much distance between me and the city guards as I could before they arrived to the sounds of the shooting.

WHEN I CAME ROUND, I was lying face down across a forest trail.

My face smarted, grazed during my fall from the horse. My broken nose was bleeding. My Horse Riding skill had deactivated in full gallop, throwing me off the horse.

Status, Wanderer
Level, 11

Luckily, my steed hadn't gone far. There it was, grazing peacefully on the fresh grass. I picked up the short cavalry musket, walked over to the horse and pulled out the two pistols from the saddle holster, just in case. I pushed them under my belt, put my foot into the stirrup, scrambled onto the horse and gave it a light nudge with my knees.

The horse trotted unhurriedly along the forest trail. For a while I rode unthinkingly until suddenly I sensed a sharp pull similar to that of a tightening fish line. This was the phantom cord connecting me to the murderer pulling at me again.

The metamorph was here somewhere. Either he, or his discarded trophy.

I climbed down the horse, very nearly collapsing in a heap on the ground. Musket at the ready, I traipsed through the forest until I came to a small hill. Once I climbed it, I saw a hunters' lodge which looked a carbon copy of the one which had started all this.

Only this time, its owner was at home. A forest ranger sat on the porch, a pitchfork pinning him to the log wall. A pool of blood had formed at his feet. The air swarmed with flies.

Neither the kidnapped boy nor the metamorph himself were around. Still, I knew they were inside. That's where the magic cord kept pulling me.

I crept down the hill and stole toward the hut. Immediately the hairy bulk of a werewolf lunged at me from out of the bushes. My Accuracy had long been gone: I wasted a bullet which missed my opponent and split a thin young fir tree instead. The level-40 werewolf growled his triumph and went for me.

The sapphire on my ring finger flashed and disintegrated, emitting a blinding white ray of light which hit the werewolf and paralyzed him, winning me a few precious seconds.

> **Needle of a Witch (single-use artifact).**
> **Attack Intensity, 60**
> **Natural immunity, 41**
> **Your defense has failed. You've been paralyzed. Duration, 19 sec**

I didn't waste time. Pulling the suddenly heavy and unyielding sword out of its scabbard, I gripped it with both my hands and brought it down onto the monster's clawed paw the way an executioner aims his axe.

The sharp blade clove through the bone with ease, the monster's black blood hissing on the Dwarven silver.

> **Damage: 150/1050**
> **Critical damage**
> **-25% to Agility**
> **Regeneration: +5% Pt. Health/sec**
> **Additional damage from silver: -4 pt. Health/sec**

The severed limb dropped to the ground,

the terrible wound emitting acidic smoke. I slashed at the creature's back leg but the sword blade barely brushed it so I had to attack him again. This time my sword lodged deep in the creature's joint. The charmed runes covering the blade began to glow, bright and fierce like the desert sun. I dealt a few more blows which completely exhausted me but at least I'd chopped through the mob's leg, leaving it hanging on a fine strip of skin.

The werewolf collapsed to one side, gradually recovering from his stupor. He snapped his greedy jaws, barely missing me. I dodged his attack and darted for the hut. The wounded werewolf was no running match: he span in place, whimpering and clawing the ground with his two surviving feet.

As I ran, my eye detected a faint shimmering haze hanging in the air. I stopped just in time and sent a quick query regarding the nature of this new anomaly. A box appeared in my mental view, reporting its damage numbers. It was over a thousand!

Had I not stopped, it would have roasted me alive.

The werewolf howled behind me. I had to activate the ring on my index finger. The magic neutralizer penetrated the charmed veil protecting the hut, smothering it until the shimmering haze flashed and exploded in a cascade of illusory glass fragments.

Still, I couldn't get inside without help from some powerful sorcery artifacts. The web of black symbols had already spread over my body, creeping up from under my collar onto my face. I had virtually no XP left, turning into a useless newb by the minute.

Status, Wanderer
Level 7

This was awful.

I didn't want to turn into a newb! This drop from the heights of my superiority to the rock bottom of helplessness was just too much to bear.

Now I wasn't even driven by the desire to save the kidnapped boy anymore. I just wanted to get to the hacker who'd had the audacity to destroy my character.

When you have nothing to lose, you can become capable of anything, no matter how stupid. So I stepped inside without even considering the consequences.

The hut turned out much bigger than it had looked from the outside. The boy lay spread-eagled at the center of the room, his wrists and ankles nailed to the floorboards with long steel spikes. A naked girl stood next to him, busy grinding the curved blade of a predatory-looking knife. She turned to the sound, raising a surprised eyebrow.

You have a real timing problem, her voice rustled in my head. As if on cue, viscous black shadows began flowing from the room's corners toward me.

Mental attack strength: 68
Immunity to powers of Inferno: 13
Immunity to hypnosis magic: 5
Class bonus: 2
Defense failed

The shadows wrapped around my legs and began climbing higher, freezing my body motionless. My numb fingers dropped the sword. In one final effort, I managed to throw my left hand overhead, activating my last ring.

The Fire of Holy Exorcism had 99 pt. Attack on it, destroying all the summoned demons and spirits. Its magic had already helped me out earlier back in the inn's cellar. Here too it did the trick, burning the shadows in its invisible glow and throwing the metamorph to the wall, contorting like a vampire impaled on a wooden stake.

The problem was, the metamorph had

failed to crumble to ashes as he was supposed to.

He hadn't even lost his footing!

Nor had he revealed his true face.

The guise he was wearing had protected him from the spell's attack, although his dead eyes were now bleeding. The seams of his patchwork skin oozed claret.

"What, is that it?" the creature snickered the moment my ring's ruby glow died. "Whatcha gonna do now, *newb*? Are you gonna laugh me to death?"

I was now level 1, the lowest in the game. I had no hope in hell of winning even the easiest of fights, luck or no luck. Still, when the metamorph finally released himself from the wall's grip, I didn't even think of fleeing. Instead, I pulled out my flint pistol.

"What is it, *lead*?" his soft laughter rustled through the air. "Please. This isn't funny anymore."

We stood barely twenty paces away from each other. The boy lying spread-eagled on the floor was even closer. At this range, a newb like myself had no chance of hitting a target. Still I drew in a slow deep breath like I did every time at the shooting range. In one smooth practiced motion I raised the pistol, pointed it at the boy's head and squeezed the trigger.

Flint grated on steel, creating a cascade of

sparks and igniting gunpowder in the priming pan. The shot resounded. In this brief moment the metamorph lunged into the ball's path trying to block it with his own body. He didn't make it. The heavy ball of lead hit Alex on the head, dashing his brains everywhere and throwing him out of the game.

"No!" the murderer yelled. "You bastard!"

His body began to grow, expanding. Its delicate girly skin split open, exposing the flesh of a demon.

"You're mine!" the monster croaked. "I'll have you wriggle at my feet for the rest of eternity, you worm!"

This I could believe. Trust this hacker to imprison me in virtual reality. He had all the power he needed to prevent me from returning to my human body.

Oh yes, I believed him all right. Which was why the moment he reached his ugly claws out to me, I whipped out the other pistol and pressed the barrel to my chin.

The sound of flint against steel, the flash of igniting gunpowder. The brief moment as I awaited death.

The murderer's eyes filled with desperate fury.

You see, players tend to become one with their virtual bodies. They forget that this is only a game. Here, death is only a technicality. Like a computer rebooting. Players do tend to cling on to their virtual lives.

Well, I didn't.

I'm not a player. Have never been one.

This is my job.

With a jolt, darkness devoured me.

Return to main menu

TRANSLATED FROM RUSSIAN BY IRENE WOODHEAD AND NEIL P. MAYHEW

Shamanic Rites

A tale from
The Way of the Shaman series

by Vasily Mahanenko

"MINDBLOWING," I muttered as I stepped onto the ship's deck. Mahan was the one who called it a ship, but it looked more like a terrible leviathan with tentacles. I could hardly imagine what the developers had in mind when they came up with THIS! The name spoke for itself—a squidolphin. Maybe it wasn't the giant one of myth...but still, it was imposing in its own right. "Never in my life would I imagine that anyone could sail in such a monster!"

"Kornik..." Mahan suddenly whispered to no one in particular, forcing me to look around. Had he hit his head during the battle? Was he talking to himself? "She is ready..."

"Are you sure?" Before I could come to a conclusion about my teacher's mental state, I heard the goblin's voice right beside me. I started from the surprise and cursed aloud. It was a good thing that the profanity filter kept anyone from hearing it. How much more of this could I take? This little green weirdo keeps popping up out of nowhere, scaring me, saying a couple phrases, smirking and vanishing. Does he want me to develop a stutter, the stunted ghoul?! I'll show him how to...But hold on! What am I ready for?

"Yes, absolutely. I don't doubt it for a second. She is ready."

"In that case...Fleita!" Kornik turned to face me and—wonder of wonders—said to me very seriously: "Come over here!"

"Kornik?" All my snark left me just like that. Now I simply wanted to know what they had in mind, so I decided to stall. What am I ready for? Where are they trying to take me? What the heck is going on here? "What are you doing here? Have you come to check out Mahan's ship as well?"

"You think I've never seen a squidolphin before? Back in the day, it was the only way to travel. We have other business at the moment. Get your things—your next trial awaits you."

"But it's still five months away!" When I realized where they were taking me, my jaw just about fell off. How could it be?! I was ready for anything but being launched into a test for my next Shamanic level. According to the manuals, it was supposed to be a long ways off.

"Your teacher says that you are ready—so you're ready. It's not up to you," sneered the green booger. Why does this NPC have such an idiotic Imitator? "Let's go. The Supreme Fire Spirit is expecting you."

"But...am I really ready, Mahan?" I made a last ditch attempt to eke out a little time. Laboring under the assumption that the trial was far off in the distant future, I hadn't prepared one bit. I needed time to familiarize myself with the manuals back in reality. And I just knew in my heart of hearts that if I accepted right now and went with Kornik, then I signing out to read up would cause me to fail the trial. I don't like to play this way!

In true Mahan fashion, he nodded and grinned in that telling, professorial manner of a teacher. I sighed deeply and clenched my fists in futile anger. The jerk! When he simply plays the game and does his quests he's nothing short of a gaming god—everything works out for him, he finds the most interesting areas, crafts the most fascinating items. But when he acts like this, like some great guru, I just want to pick up something with good heft and lower it onto his head while screaming at him to stop being such a moron! He acts like a little child! Some Shaman...!

I was feeling quite down by this point, so I didn't say anything as I took Kornik's hand and in a blink of an eye was transported from my teacher's ship to somewhere deep in the mountains. A biting cold washed over me, but I ignored it. I bet I'll get sick and die young! Then that jerk will regret his stupid smile!

"Whom did you bring, brother?" sounded a bombastic voice from all around us.

"I have brought a Seeker. She is on the

path to find herself and it is our duty to aid her," replied the goblin.

"But is she ready?"

"No one but the Spirit of the Forest knows this."

"Will she manage?"

"No one but the Spirit of the Mountains has this knowledge."

What drivel! Mommy birth me back into non-existence! Why oh why are all Shamans such helpless fools?! What is all this dramatic posturing for? Why can't you simply say: 'Fleita, here's the cave of trials. Do this and that, go here and there, get that thing, and push the green button.' Why all the mumbo jumbo? Why couldn't Mahan warn me about the trial? Tell me about it? Can't the blind ass see that I like him?

"Bow your head, little sister," Kornik said triumphantly, having finished his spiel with the 'all-knowing Spirits.' "You are in the presence of the Great Spirit of Fire, what has come to witness your initiation."

I glanced sullenly at the whirlwind that had appeared beside us and raised my chin proudly, not even contemplating bending my knee. This is a game, and I'm the one in charge here! If some NPC wants me to bow, then good luck to him in such a futile endeavor!

"You are ready!" the Spirit droned in a low

bass. Shivers ran down my spine from his words, but I didn't lower my chin a millimeter. Not a chance! "To become a Beginner Shaman, you must prove that your spirit is steadfast, that your spirit is pliant, that your spirit is strong, that your spirit is gentle. You must enter the cave, where four trials await you. What you do with each—is a choice that your spirit makes, let it guide you. If you fail even one trial, your initiation shall be postponed. In your case, for six months. Every shaman has the chance to become a Harbinger, but not all take this path. It is up to you alone whether you become a real Shaman.

Quest chain received: 'The Way of the Shaman.'
'The Way of the Shaman: Step 1.' Complete the labyrinth of trials.
0 of 4 trials completed (next attempt in 180 days).

"Enter the cave and trust your spirit. It will help you make the correct decision."

The air began to spin around me, raising the dust that was normally absent in Barliona. When the lightshow ended, I found myself in a cave with four passages, marked with the digits one through four. A notification immediately appeared before my eyes:

Information for the player! You have started 'The Way of the Shaman: Step 1' Quest. You have two attempts for completing this trial. If you fail, you can attempt the trial again in a month's time. If your first attempt fails, press the red stone by the entrance to start your second attempt. Have a pleasant game!

Finally! At long last a clear explanation in this entire circus! I will have two attempts to pass the trial without a time limit, although I still had a hunch that I wouldn't be allowed to log out into reality. On the other hand, I'll be able to check the forums and manuals...or call Mahan and tell him what I think of him! I think that's where I'll start!

To my astonishment, my amulet didn't work here, so my teacher was spared the happy news of what kind of lowlife I thought he was. It's odd—I don't recall ever being so angry with anyone. I had grown attached to this Shaman as of late, and it was difficult to admit to myself that he had rejected me so easily and sent me out to swim on my own...Jerk! The forums on the other hand brought happier tidings: Players who had undergone the trial before me detailed exactly what they had done to complete it. It consisted of four rooms with a particular scenario in each and you simply had to do certain things to complete each one. That's it. Nothing too complicated, nothing too terrifying.

The first room was divided in half by a partition. One side of the partition contained a hole, from where a fawn's head was sticking out, while the other contained a wolf. The wolf was growling with his fangs bared. His paw was caught in a bear trap. According to the forum threads, the challenge here was simple: This was a test of your gentleness of Spirit. You had to take out the fawn and leave the room without a second thought. However, just as I was about to approach the trapped animal, I was struck by the feeling that this whole scenario was wrong and stopped in my tracks.

It can't be this simple!

I sat down on the floor and began to think. The fire whirlwind had mentioned that I would need to trust my spirit and Mahan had kept his own experience with the trial secret from me. On the forum, the players all complained that none of them had managed to make it to Harbinger. It's been two weeks since Sergei has come by to hang out with me and my girlfriends are saying that they've seen him out and about with Katie— that plucked chicken! Meanwhile, Mahan is acting like he doesn't notice the attention I give him. Besides, the weather outside is awful so there's no point going out tonight…

Damn it all! They can all go take a walk! Aren't I a Zombie after all?

I jumped to my feet and examined first the fawn, then the wolf. If I save the first, the other will perish. If I save the other—the first will perish. So let both of them perish!

Two quick summons of the Spirits sent both the wolf and the fawn to the afterlife, if this game even has one of those. Someone wants me to listen to my spirit? All right! Just don't act shocked when what follows isn't to your liking! What I liked about playing as a Zombie was the ability to temporarily raise pets from the dead. If you kill a creature, you can resurrect it and spend an hour adventuring with it—until it falls apart to pieces. It's a useful trick at the lower levels, since you get the XP from the pet's kills. But the best thing is that the undead pet forgets all about its former existence—fears, desires and all—and is fully in the player's power!

I had never raised two creatures from the dead before and had to concentrate extra hard to do it now. It was worth it however. I emerged from the first room with the fawn and the wolf jerking and twitching like marionettes on my leash. Maybe they weren't alive or very healthy, but at least they moved. And who cares if I wasn't supposed to be doing this. Even if I fail now, I'll still have another attempt.

Quest update: 'The Way of the Shaman (Step 1)': 1 of 4 trials completed.

The second trial consisted of an ordinary five-meter-wide pit filled with water. A thin rope spanned the pit. For whatever reason, the players on the forums called this a bridge. The challenge was simple—I had to get to the other side. The proper way to do it was to calm myself and swim across the obstacle, but my agitation from the earlier trial had not subsided.

As Mahan likes to say: Yeah right! I am a Zombie. I am a Shaman. And I have two undead pets that will be dead within the hour one way or another. Why shouldn't they lend me a helping paw?

It was practically impossible to walk along the rope to the other side, especially considering my sense of balance. Or rather, my utter lack thereof. And I didn't feel like jumping in the water, so I did that which no Shaman before me could have done—I dismembered the fawn and the wolf into their constituent limbs.

To walk along the rope, I would need to hold onto something with my hands. I didn't have a second rope, but I did now have fresh, strong bones from my two zombie pets. It's not like their ultimate death would matter to them much.

Neither the wolf nor the fawn made a sound as I broke off the bones from their bodies and bound them together with the veins and sinews. Surprisingly, the typically kind and wonderful Barliona did not interfere with such maniacal treatment of its creatures. I only hoped that when I returned to reality, I wouldn't find orderlies in white scrubs waiting at the capsule to take me to the asylum. The Corporation could easily pull something like that.

Tossing the fawn's and wolf's heads into my bag (if only to get them out of my sight), I cast my improvised pole of bones to the other side of the pit and looked on with astonishment when the far end fused seamlessly with the edge. It was as if someone had anticipated precisely this solution. Humming to myself, I fixed my end of the pole to the floor and carefully shuffling my feet began to shimmy along the bridge. I was a bit surprised to find that I felt no revulsion from touching the snow white bones I was using to support myself. My mind had shut off. I was operating purely on emotion, like Mahan had taught me.

The jerk!

Quest update: 'The Way of the Shaman (Step 1)': 2 of 4 trials completed.

In the third room I found ten human statues made of stone with clubs in their hands. This was a test for the strength of spirit. I had to walk through the statues (that the forums had named 'the ancestors') while ignoring the blows they'd deal me. What madness. No one in their right mind would take damage voluntarily. Even if the assailant happens to be your grandpa, grandma and uncle all at once! Even at the setting my sensory filter was set to...

Stop! How can a Zombie have ancestors anyway?! And why do they resemble humans? Where are the Zombie orcs, goblins and elves? Where is it all? It's simply not there! In that case, these aren't the ancestors of my race! These are simply statues of stone that want to hammer on my back with their clubs.

Thanks, but no thanks.

Since it was dangerous to approach the statues, I took the fawn and wolf heads out of my bag and placed them on the floor—and thanked my gym teacher for being such a staunch soccer fan. In class, he taught everyone regardless of gender how to properly kick the ball and do it precisely. I never imagined that the skills I learned in gym class would come in handy in Barliona, but life was funny that way.

A kick!

The wolf's head slammed into the nearest

statue with a dull *thwack*, smashing it to dust. I was about to pat myself on the back for finding yet another way to avoid taking damage when a ghost materialized where the statue had been. White and transparent he looked like he was bellowing at me enraged, though I couldn't hear a thing. Anyway, he didn't actually move in my direction, so I relaxed. After kicking the fawn's head into the second statue, I confirmed that the first ghost's appearance hadn't been a one-off thing. The second disembodied spirit was also screaming and cursing, but we remained in separate planes of reality. In that case, I couldn't care less! Picking up the wolf's head that had rolled back to me, I took aim at the third statue. This was turning into a fun game!

Quest update: 'The Way of the Shaman (Step 1)': 3 of 4 trials completed.

For whatever reason, the developers seemed to imagine steadfastness of spirit as a heap of rice and peas. According to the rules, I was supposed to sort this heap into two halves, receive my Totem and rejoice in my new Shamanic class. Squatting down, I took a minute to establish that I wasn't much for playing Cinderella. The very idea of how dull and long the task before me was made me want to pass out. I mean, even my hands were falling asleep, the fingers nodding off...No, this couldn't go on. I would never manage to sort this whole heap on my own.

I went back to the hall with the second trial and picked up the rod of bone. After wasting another twenty minutes in futile attempts to raise the wolf and fawn from the dead again, I gave up, tossed the bones into my bag and swore loudly. The profanity filter silenced my words yet again, so from the perspective of my surroundings I remained sitting in front of a heap of peas and rice, staring at it like I'd never seen rice and peas before. Am I really going to have to do this on my own?

Yeah right! Oh man, Mahan had really made this phrase stick in my head.

The ghosts in the third hall hadn't left. They remained in their original places slinging soundless oaths against this living world. I walked up to one of them and noticed that he was standing on a small plinth. I prodded it with the wolf's shinbone and couldn't help but exclaim with joy—the plinth moved aside, dragging the ghost with it! Perfect! I know exactly who's going to sort that heap for me!

I spent the next five minutes pushing the plinths with their ghosts to the last room. The ghosts tried to grab me, but we were still in separate planes of existence and their hands simply passed through me. I just hoped that they wouldn't do the same with the peas and rice! Having arranged the plinths around the heap, I couldn't think of anything better than to point at it and say:

"I need that sorted. Get on with it!"

I knew the ghosts had heard me because their faces stretched in astonishment, while the only woman among them dropped her jaw and gaped at me. Well, at least they'd cut out their (soundless) clamor!

"Why are you just standing there? Who are you waiting for? I said, this pile needs to be sorted! Rice to one side, peas to the other! Let's go people! Don't make me wait!"

Haltingly, as if he couldn't believe what he was doing, one of the ghosts squatted down, reached for the heap and—miracle of miracles—picked up one pea and placed it aside. Then another one. And another. By and by, the other 'ancestors,' whom I think I was supposed to be venerating, joined the first ghost. Well in my view, there's no greater form of veneration than teamwork. What could be more venerable?

"Wonderful!" I said, ecstatic, when the last pea had reached its proper heap. "Now you're free to go!"

"This is an outrage!" yelled one of the

ghosts. I stared at him in shock—I could hear him! "I wasn't a mighty arch-mage in my former life to sort peas for some petulant girl!"

"I am not petulant!" I parried, realizing too late that in doing so I was letting the ghosts know that I could hear them...As if they were waiting for this, they all now began to yell at me, curse me with unprintable words, and threaten me with terrible tortures and retributions. I clapped my hands over my ears and yet even then I could hear them raving, so that finally pushed to the brink, I grabbed a pail of water (by the way, where had it come from anyway?) and dump it onto the ghosts. Let them cool off a bit!

The water swept through the ghosts, doing them no harm at all, and fell onto the heap of rice, scattering it in every direction. I dropped the pail—damn! Taking the bones and using them as a shovel, I began to sweep the rice back into its heap—I still had to complete the trial. The ghosts fell silent and watched me work, or perhaps they didn't wish to be noticed to keep me from forcing them to work again. I'll deal with them later though—at the moment, I need to gather the rice back into its heap.

I was about to celebrate my progress when one of the platforms began to shake. I stared at it puzzled and saw several grains of rice on it covered in dust. They were steadily growing into the platform, cracking it in half. Several moments passed and a green shoot appeared, decked in pretty flowers. The platform, meanwhile, was broken. With a drawn out groan, one of the ghosts was sucked into a flower, and here I became aware of similar groans coming from all around me—all of the platforms had been destroyed by the rice, while all the ghists were sucked into the flowers that had appeared.

Without thinking, I reached out and touched one of the flowers. Its tip opened like a bulb revealing the projection of a small bear cub. He was so adorable, cute and clumsy that my teeth went on edge as if I'd eaten too much sugar. My gawd! Cuteness overload! My classmates would be losing their minds from happiness, seeing such a miracle. And yet the only thing I felt was loathing. I don't like bears! The next bulb unfurled to reveal a wolf, the next a bunny, then a panther, a snake, a crow...Ten cute critters that elicited nothing from me but a deep sigh. What is this supposed to be? The ghosts had turned into animals? And what am I supposed to do with them?

Overcoming my disgust, I forced myself to pet the wolf cub. Yes, he was soft. Yes, he was pretty cool. Yes, he was so cute that you wanted to press him to yourself and never let him go, and yet when the next notification appeared before me, I staggered back from the flower with the wolf cub like from a fire:

Quest received: 'Searching for your Totem'. You have chosen your Totem: Gray Wolf. In order to begin your search, speak to your Shaman teacher.

So this is the Totem? No! I don't want my Totem to be a Wolf! I want my Totem to be a Dragon, like Mahan's! Give me a Dragon!

But there was no Dragon among the ten flowers. There were bunnies, squirrels, wolves and other denizens of the forest—but no Dragon.

I don't play like that!

Sitting down on the ground, I began to scan the forums again—to little avail. No one on the forum had been able to choose their Totem. The system had made the decision for them. I was already a black sheep in this regard...by the way, I think I saw a black lamb among the flowers...

No! I want a Dragon! And I will have one too!

I dumped the bones from my bag onto the floor and began to think. Only recently I had failed at re-raising the fawn and wolf from the dead. Something hadn't jelled. But it's not like I needed it to anymore. What I needed now was something entirely different—something that Barliona had never seen before...

I needed to make myself a Dragon, even if he would be made of nothing but bone.

Let's get to it then.

I didn't have anything to bind the bones with, so I shamelessly pulled up the shoots of rice, stripped off and cast aside the bulbs with their cute critters and used the stems as bindings. The Dragon turned out scary looking and bore no resemblance to Mahan's Totem whatsoever, but that didn't stop me. I knew what I wanted!

I'd have a Dragon of my own, or my name isn't Fleite!

Quest update: 'Searching for your Totem': You have changed your Totem from Gray Wolf to Undead Bone Dragon. In order to begin your search, speak to your Shaman teacher.

Quest completed: 'The Way of the Shaman: Step 1.'

TRANSLATED FROM RUSSIAN BY BORIS SMIRNOV

Purgatory

A TALE FROM
PHANTOM SERVER AND *CRYSTAL SPHERE*
SERIES

BY ANDREI LIVADNY

THEY WERE TWENTY: THE FIRST HUMANS TO
TRANSCEND REALITY.
THIS IS THE STORY OF ONLY ONE OF THEM.

DIETRICH WASN'T THAT WORRIED about the trial. He'd lived a long and not exactly sheltered life with its fair share of problems and vagaries; he knew what it could throw at him and was pretty sure he'd come out clean. He had plenty of money; the rest was paperwork. He'd been through worse.

"And?" he looked up sharply at his lawyer, annoyed by his sullen silence.

"They're offering you a deal."

"How much?"

"This time it's not about money, Mr. Craw. I'm afraid they got you this time."

"Keep it short."

'They're willing to commute the cryo repository into a week of virtual incarceration."

"What's the catch?" Dietrich leaned back in the uncomfortable chair, locked his fingers and squinted at his lawyer. "So they won't deep freeze me but send me to cyberspace instead?"

"You'll have to have a neuroimplant installed."

"What the hell is that?"

"From what I've managed to find out, it's an artificial neural network. It connects to your brain and feeds it with an entire range of perceptions, allowing you to experience everything as if it were the real world."

"Never heard of it. Is it dangerous?"

The lawyer shrugged. "It's either cryo or cyberspace. You choose. To be completely honest with you, I just can't see any other option in this situation. For some reason unbeknown to me your case has attracted the interest of both the space forces and the world's biggest gaming corporation. All your connections aren't worth jack against that kind of folk. Your bank accounts have also been seized."

Dietrich frowned.

He had nothing to do with gaming. Or virtual realities. So far, his life had been strictly real. He'd never had the time to waste on all that nonsense. "Just spit it out! Quit pussyfooting around, for crissakes! What's the catch?"

"I personally think they're testing these things. It's new technology. What they call cutting-edge science. Can you imagine the sense of danger some in-game monsters can instill in a player? If my information is correct and those neuroimplants can indeed feed an entire range of perceptions to the brain, you could very easily die with pain when you get 'killed' in virtual reality."

Dietrich frowned, thinking. If that's what they wanted, they were making a big mistake. He was good at pain. The metropolis had never been nice to him. Born in the gutter, he'd made his way to the top all by himself. "A week, you say? Any guarantees?"

"It's a proper deal. If nothing irrevocable happens, after seven days they'll drop all charges against you."

Dietrich nodded. The legal system had outsmarted itself this time. So they expected him to curl up and die? They thought he wouldn't make it? Well, that remained to be seen.

His lips curved in a smirk. "Give it to me, I'll sign it. You make sure that in seven days I get my due welcome."

✳ ✳ ✳

"WHY WOULD YOU even need convicts? This is something I don't understand!" the Infosystems Corporation production engineer cringed. "If you as much as hint at the new equipment's authenticity levels, you'll have millions of gamers lining up outside the door! We're making the game of the future! Why would we need to-"

"Dietrich Craw is perfect for our purposes," the space forces representative replied calmly. "This technology has an incredible potential, Jurgen. Which means we need to study all of its possible sides. Dark ones, as well," he added, deadpan serious. "Don't you remember what happened during the last series of tests?"

The engineer waved his question away. "Just

a glitch. We've already found the problem and fixed it."

"Which was what, character generation by the user's mind? How's that for a glitch? You need to study it and then decide whether to use it or lose it."

"It's against all gaming principles!" Jurgen snapped. "If every user begins to generate new characters, items and events from their own memory, all hell will break loose!"

"I agree. But there're other ways we could use this. In any case, we can't ignore the latest results. We have a precedent which needs to be properly studied. Have you ever thought that the recreation of one's mental images in virtual reality might be the first step toward immortality?"

"Then we're aren't going to run him through the mob gauntlet?"

"No. But we might push the envelope a little... just to see how far the neuroimplant can go."

Jurgen leafed through the paperwork. "In that case we'll need a few more test subjects," he pointed out.

"That's not a problem."

✳ ✳ ✳

DIETRICH HAD PUT the seventy-two hours that had elapsed between his signing the deal and the beginning of his seven-day "virtual stint" (as he'd nicknamed the upcoming adventure) to good use. He'd asked for *A Guide Book to Virtual Worlds* and perused it diligently to find out what he'd be dealing with.

The night had left him strangely exhausted. His eyelids had grown heavy. An unconscious slumber enshrouded his mind with darkness.

He awoke in a very strange place indeed.

A bleak landscape stretched to the horizon: a flat plain without a single trace of life or vegetation, cracked and scorched by some fierce ancient fires.

He jumped to his feet and looked around him. Same thing. This didn't look like a newb location at all. Wasn't a new player supposed to enter a game via one of those?

Weird digital codes flashed before his eyes, overlapping the view. A few interface icons appeared in his mind's eye. A soft voice said,

"You've received a new ability: Absolute Memory.

You've received a new ability: Dream Come True.

The world around you is adaptable. You

73

can create certain objects or events by willing them to life, but only those familiar to you from real life."

So that's how it was, then? No manual had mentioned anything like that.

He couldn't see any mobs. Nor the sun. The air was permeated by a ubiquitous soft light. He was neither hot nor cold; he was puzzled.

He soon overcame his initial confusion. Not having gaming experience, he saw no point in moving anywhere or looking for anyone, let alone "creating" anything. They could stuff their adaptable world where the sun didn't shine.

Dietrich slumped on the scorched ground. The wisest thing was probably to do nothing at all.

He didn't last long, though. First he grew bored. Then he was thirsty. Finally, he felt hungry.

His sensations were perfectly real, he had to give them that. His physical body was taken good care of, anyway. So he braved it through until a new system message came up,

You're thirsty. You lose 1% Life every hour.
You're hungry. Your Strength has dropped 1 point.

He was parched. His throat rasped. The little

red bar in his view had indeed shrunk a little. A quick calculation told him that if it went on like that, he'd die of dehydration within the next seventy-two hours — or even earlier if the *debuffs* (he proudly used the newly-learned word) he'd received grew exponentially.

"All right, all right," he grumbled. He could use a walk, if only to stretch his legs. He might also find some food and water.

The lifeless landscape was exhausting in its monotony. Wherever you turned, it was all the same. Dietrich quickly lost track of time and the distance he'd covered. He wasn't used to walking for so long, growing more tired with every passing minute.

Was he completely alone here?

They've given you those abilities, his inner voice stealthily suggested.

"So how do you want me to use them?" Dietrich found arguing with his imaginary self quite entertaining.

Try and make some food.

He stopped. A skeptical grin touched his lips. A true citizen of an urbanized technogenic world, he had no idea where food came from. What did its source even look like?

His imagination helpfully offered him a view of a familiar automatic restaurant he used to frequent. Obeying his thoughts, the earth parted, pushing out part of a building.

He recoiled in surprise but quickly pulled himself together.

So this was their famed adaptivity, was it?

Admittedly his first spontaneous attempt to will something to life was rather average. The fragment of a city tower looked rather ugly, consisting of only one story covered with dust and listing to one side, its walls running with cracks of unknown origin. Two holographic signs blinked over the restaurant's entrance,

SYNTHIZE
IN BUSINESS WORLDWIDE

Well, let's take a look.

He headed for the entrance. The automatic doors didn't react to his approach.

"What's wrong with them?" he wondered out loud.

The immobile door halves resisted his efforts. Finally he lost patience and imagined they were simply not there. The doors disintegrated into nothing.

He entered, noticing in surprise how reality promptly changed everywhere he looked as if the game processed his mind's images, using them to recreate the restaurant's familiar interior.

Tables and chairs appeared out of nowhere,

bathed in the same soft diffused light. The bar arched along the far wall, complete with a 'droid barman. Still, on closer inspection all the objects turned out to be dummies made of some compressed gray substance. The robot didn't move. None of the automated service lines worked. All the plates and cups crumbled to dust in his hands.

He ambled aimlessly from one table to the next but found nothing of any interest. Nothing he could use; nothing that actually worked. Disgusted, he exited his failed creation and stopped nearby, pondering over the situation.

Some game they'd made! This didn't look like entertainment at all. More like a sick joke.

His hunger had subsided somewhat. His thirst, however, kept growing.

He spent the next few hours experimenting. Now he was surrounded by dummies: a tiny lake, its water as hard as glass; a small area of a park overgrown with plastic greenery — everything he'd managed to visualize or imagine had ultimately turned out to be stage props which copied the objects' form but not their purpose.

Feeling quite annoyed, Dietrich noticed the change in his surroundings. It had grown noticeably darker: a weird twilight as if cyberspace was reacting to his state of mind. Swirls of ashen dust began to follow him, growing in synch with his anger.

You're getting tired. You're so hungry and thirsty that you're now losing 3% Life every hour.

He slumped onto a bench in the park he'd just built. *This is only a game. A stupid game that I'm supposed to test. In reality, there's no danger to me whatsoever.*

His mind seemed to be living a life of its own. Half-forgotten images from the past kept surfacing as if the neuroimplant was sifting through his memories, bringing up everything he'd been trying to forget. The darkness grew thicker, forming the outlines of buildings and streets.

He shook his head free from unwelcome reminiscences and concentrated on more pressing problems. How could he get hold of some water?

Suddenly it dawned on him. He needed rain! What could be easier?

True, water falling from the sky promised nothing good to a metropolis dweller. It was nothing but urban emissions condensed into toxic clouds. Acid rain was commonplace. Still, Dietrich remembered the pure rain of his childhood when you could go out into an open-air park and where the taste of rainwater on your lips hadn't been lethal.

So this reality *was* adaptive, after all! He watched in surprise as the gloom began to transform, obeying his mental image's command. Heavy clouds gathered overhead; a clap of thunder echoed from afar. The first raindrops fell to the parched ground, rolling together like dust-covered drops of mercury.

Dietrich offered his hands up to the fresh downpour not even noticing the buildings' outlines approach, more material with every moment, until they formed a fragment of a street.

The water turned out slightly salty but he gulped it down greedily, ignoring the pinkish trickle that ran down his wrists.

Only after having drunk his fill, did he finally realize something was wrong. He glanced at his hands and cussed.

Blood? Where could it have come from? I hadn't hurt myself, had I?

He suppressed a gag, then looked around himself. The weather was getting worse by the minute. The rain pelted down, concealing the buildings' outlines. Bolts of lightning alone ripped through the dark, briefly illuminating his surroundings.

In the deadly light of a new flash Dietrich watched one of the ashen swirls take human shape.

A skinny youngster, his face a bloodied mess, his broken right arm hanging lifelessly.

In real life, Dietrich had never been afraid of

anyone but now he broke out in a cold sweat. The phantom figure stepped toward him, gaining detail, apparently trying to say something. Froth bubbled on the creature's bloodied lips; his throat gargled and wheezed.

Now Dietrich recognized him. Instinctively he recoiled, looking around. He remembered the street.

He'd wanted his childhood back, the idiot! A flash of unwelcome memories electrocuted him, paralyzing his brain.

So we're thirsty, are we? His inner voice was now mocking, sarcastic, apparently wanting Dietrich to remember himself as a fifteen-year-old kid and bring back the day when he'd first learned to solve his problems, becoming the alpha dog in a gang of equally underage hoods.

"Do you... remember me?" the phantom wheezed.

"Piss off!"

The phantom didn't obey. On the contrary: the more Dietrich concentrated on him, the more real he looked. "Fuck off!"

The rain pelted down. More ashen swirls began coming to life, transforming into the people he'd long forgotten — whose images he'd buried shamelessly within the deepest recesses of his memory. It's human nature to come up with lies in order to justify one's actions: *I simply had no choice; there was no other way; I did the right thing.*

Over time, those painful memories had faded, replaced by fresher and more vivid ones. This was the way he'd lived his life.

Damn their absolute memory! He'd always lived by the "*Death solves all problems*" adage. How many more incidents like these were stored in the recesses of his mind? No idea. Was he supposed to face all of them now?

Seven days! He wouldn't last an hour!

Desperate, Dietrich looked around himself as more and more ashen swirls rose into the air, crowding him out.

Spending his brief prison term stuck in his own personal hell was the last thing he needed. He had no desire to tick off his mortal sins as he studied the scabby scars covering his conscience.

He'd have loved to remember something positive and uplifting, something *good* — but all his life until now had been one long, unscrupulous and bloodied path to the top toward wealth, power and fleeting prosperity.

He knew this was only his neuroimplant reading his memory like an open book. The phantoms surrounding him didn't exist. Still, how was he supposed to get rid of them? Was he really so powerless?

Thoughts came in fits and starts as he kept sinking into this purgatory, recognizing more faces and recalling the events they triggered.

The teenager whose name he'd never known — the one who'd been beaten to death — got to him first. Wheezing, he reached out his good hand, clutching at Dietrich's clothes and leaving bloodied handprints which the rain didn't seem to wash away.

Dietrich recoiled but he had nowhere to retreat to anymore. Phantoms had closed in, surrounding him.

He couldn't think straight. Rage enveloped his mind in a crimson haze. He had no wish to control himself anymore. His old instincts kicked back in.

You'll all be dead in a moment!

Uncontrollable fury flooded his mind. His hand closed around something cold and heavy. The first and only item he'd as yet managed to will to life was a sharp dagger — a winning argument in this fight with his own past.

He invested all his strength into the blow. The phantom rippled, surging with interference, but Dietrich couldn't stop himself anymore. He kept stabbing the air in silent rage, feeling his fear subside. Thoughts began to fade; a viscous darkness thickened around him, devouring his mind.

In a flash of agony, the world disappeared.

✳ ✳ ✳

"HIS IDENTITY MATRIX has been stabilized. Vital functions return to normal."

Finally the classified lab's medical and neurotech staff could breathe a sigh of relief.

"Good job, guys," the military representative said, checking the subject's biometric data.

"Allow me to point out, Sir, that the subject is completely burned out."

"What do you mean?"

"His metabolism has accelerated beyond all human endurance. He's lost fifteen pounds in less than five minutes. His brain has suffered a massive loss of nervous cells. I don't think he'll survive another immersion."

"That shouldn't worry you," the military representative said. "This is a convict who's paying the price for his crimes. We will continue with the project."

Jurgen cast him an unfriendly glance. "There's no need to. We've received extensive data proving that the neuroimplant in its current form is unfit for human use. The risks are too high. This technology is lethal. No one's gonna opt for this kind of immortality. We all have our skeletons in our closets."

"It's a good job you're not in charge. It's not your decision."

"But it's my job as an expert to write the implant's assessment."

"If it's for your corporation, be my guest."

"We're supposed to create the game of the future," Jurgen insisted. "Its absolute authenticity is its main selling point. The implant is supposed to offer experiences identical to the player's actions in the game, not to pull ghosts out of his past!"

"You'd better get back to work then, hadn't you? You need to go through all the spectrum of potential effects on the subject's mind and choose those suitable for use in the game. The Infosystems Corporation agreed to purchase a truncated version of the neuroimplant which would only serve the game's purposes."

Jurgen preserved a moody silence, studying the schemes. Finally, he overcame his resentment, "Mind telling me where you got this technology from? Somehow I don't think you developed it from scratch."

"Mind your own business," the military representative snapped. "Ask no questions, tell no lies. Unless you want to become the next test subject."

He switched on the intercom. "You can get our man ready," he spoke into the microphone. "Identity matrix upload in one hour. Make sure he knows his cover story."

✳ ✳ ✳

DIETRICH HAD no idea how long he'd been in pain. Finally, the agony subsided. The crimson haze before his eyes began to dissipate, revealing the same old drab landscape.

But the phantoms were gone. Ditto for the clumsy street setting. Instead, a man was sitting on a boulder nearby, chewing on a twig and staring at the caked ground, looking utterly bored.

For a while, Dietrich watched the stranger surreptitiously. He was short and stocky, about thirty years old, with a round and good-natured rosy-cheeked face. His clothes were rather plain. He'd never met anyone like him before, that's for sure. He couldn't have anything to do with the ghosts of his past. Which was good news even though it didn't explain where he'd come from or what he needed here. Had he been waiting for Dietrich to come round?

"What do you want?" Dietrich croaked, trying to scramble back to his feet. His head spun, sending him reeling. After everything that had happened to him, he expected another catch.

He was wrong though.

The stranger didn't show any signs of aggression. His gaze was filled with respectful disapproval. "You're strong but stupid," he said. "If you go on like this, you won't last long."

"Why, what have I done?"

"You've probably destroyed one or two of your own memories by the looks of it. Am I right?"

Dietrich pricked up his ears. "Is that possible?"

The stranger chuckled. "It's easier than you think. Not recommended for frequent use, though. Trust me."

"Why not?"

"Not a healthy idea. Memories are part of your identity. By destroying them, you're destroying yourself."

"Bullshit! I've lived all my life without them. Couldn't have been better."

"That's what you think. The human brain doesn't forget anything. It's just that we normally try not to rake up the past."

"What's your name again?" Dietrich mumbled, trying to change the subject.

"Rich."

"So what do you want, Rich?"

"Just passing by. Saw you lying here unconscious. We don't have many newbs here. I was curious."

"Are there many other convicts here?"

Rich arched a surprised eyebrow. "Not that I know of."

"Do you mean you're here of your own free will?"

"Sure. Earning my bit on the side. They pay good money for implant testing. The contract is a bastard though. I'm stuck here for another six months. They block your logout the moment you enter."

"What is this place, anyway? Can you tell me?"

"This? This is the Infosystems Corporation testing grounds," Rich replied eagerly as he created a table with two easy chairs. "Come and take a seat. And give it a break, will you? Of course I'm interested in you. We might do a bit of trading. But first I need to explain something to you."

Unwilling to give him the impression of being paranoid, Dietrich took one of the chairs. He didn't believe in good Samaritans. Still, it would be stupid to pass by the rare chance of getting some information on board.

"Spit it out," he said.

Rich cast a wary look around, then leaned closer to him. A plastic water bottle materialized on the table. "Help yourself. I can see you could use a drink. It's against the rules but I don't think they'll notice. Consider it a gesture of good will."

Dietrich didn't have to ask himself twice. His life bar had already shrunk to half its original size. He was parched, too.

The water turned out to be fresh and clear. He'd only taken a few swigs when a new system message appeared,

You're not thirsty anymore. Your Health is restoring.

"Why did you think they wouldn't notice?" he asked.

"You should keep an eye on the sky. If you notice a thin purple strip running across it, that's them doing the scanning. Then you should be careful. They won't punish you for something petty like this. Still, better to be safe than sorry."

The moment Dietrich finished the water, the bottle disappeared.

"If I understand correctly, you're a convict?" Rich asked.

"Yeah. Seven days. My lawyer made a deal," Dietrich chose to tell him the truth.

"I see now. They didn't tell you anything, did they? I can see all the twisters swirling around you."

"Is it bad?"

"Bad memories, yeah. Good ones manifest themselves differently. Like a gentle warm breeze or a ray of sunlight. It depends."

"What am I supposed to do with them?"

"Just accept them. If you want to survive, that is. This place is like purgatory."

"Are you suggesting I have to spend a week in

my personal hell surrounded by ghosts?"

"Why, is it so bad? Your past, I mean?"

Dietrich frowned. "You could say that. Never mind. I'll sort it all out. Now tell me why you came. What kind of trading do you mean? Water? Food? I've nothing to offer you. How did you make the water, by the way?"

"Easy. You need to visualize any kind of plastic container, then add its chemical formula to the image. Same with water. Just add H_2O and you have it."

"All I've managed to make is some gray powder. Everything made of it immediately crumbles to dust. How am I supposed to know chemical formulas? What a bunch of morons! I was told they were making a new game. That's bullshit! A game should make money! And this," Dietrich swept his hand around, barely missing a few of the noticeably grown ash twisters, "this is crap! You think someone's gonna pay for this?"

"Quit belly-aching," Rich replied calmly. "They *are* making a new game, don't you worry. I even know what they want to call it: Phantom Server. Both interaction and authenticity levels are going to be out of this world. And this place, if you absolutely need to know, is where they test neuroimplants. They want to find out what an artificial neural network can and can't do. This technology is new. They're obliged to make it difficult and set all sorts of non-game tasks."

This didn't sound good. Surviving these seven days might turn out to be a job and a half. "Okay," Dietrich said. "You're the smartass. You know formulas and stuff. Think you can make a simple object?"

"Depends what it is."

Dietrich willed the table top to become soft and malleable. With a few practiced motions, he scratched a scheme of the desired object upon its surface.

Rich paused, thinking. "I can do it," he finally said. "But," he leaned back in his seat, "I told you you shouldn't take risks."

"Why not?" Dietrich insisted.

"All right, I'll explain. If you can't work it out yourself, listen to me. When you were a child, you learned to recognize objects, colors and images. When you grew up a little, you began accumulating experiences. Your identity is in fact based on your memory which in turn is just a sequence of smaller separate memories. Good ones, bad ones, all sorts. You get my point?"

"Not really."

"If you keep getting rid of your memories, you'll destroy yourself. Your identity will crumble like a house of cards."

Dietrich winced. "Was that why it hurt so much when I killed that scumbag?"

"I don't know who you're talking about but it does hurt, yes. If your life hasn't been too charitable, you'll have plenty of nasty ghosts to handle. Just don't think you can find peace by destroying them."

"I told you I'd sort it out. Just name your price. What do you want in return?"

"Well," Rich faltered, "to put it bluntly, all of us used to have a life and an objective. We all had to sacrifice a lot on our way to our goals. And here, all of a sudden it becomes a problem. Here you just can't experience something you've never had. You can't use something you know nothing about. You know what I mean?"

"I think so."

"Right. How was your sex life?"

Dietrich didn't know what to say. He expected anything but that.

"All right, all right, let me explain," Rich said. "You shouldn't get any ideas. You see, all my life has been strictly professional. On one hand, this was good. Now that I have the neuroimplant, I can do lots of things thanks to my old skills. But I've never been a ladies' man. It never seemed to quite work out. I never thought it mattered anyway. Not compared to my career and stuff."

"What did you do then?"

"I was an engineer in a space settlement."

"With Space Forces?"

"Yeah. Don't ask why they got rid of me. The fact remains I missed out on lots of things in life. And here it makes me feel inadequate."

"What have I got to do with it?"

"I repeat the question. How often did you have sex?"

This time Dietrich replied without embarrassment, "More often than I'd like to admit."

"That's good," Rich said. "If you give me a couple of your memories, that'll allow me to... to fill in the gap."

"Be my guest. I have tons of them. But how are we supposed to do the swap? Didn't you just say I should take good care of my memories?"

"A swap is not the same as a kill. It doesn't hurt. There'll be no damage to your identity provided you have plenty left as you've just said."

"Okay. What do I get in return?"

"How about this?" Rich pointed at the clumsy drawing of a gun scratched into the tabletop. "A pulse Steiger, good enough?"

"Including some spare batteries, the ammo's technical description and its chemical formula so I could make it myself," Dietrich said unflinchingly. He wasn't worried about the task's potential complexity. Hadn't they said he'd been granted absolute memory? "Plus some food and water."

Rich frowned, thinking, then stated, "In that case I want two memories, complete with every detail."

"Not a problem. It's a deal. Only I don't quite understand how we're supposed to make the swap."

"You need to concentrate on a couple of the more vivid memories, then will me to have them."

"Should I maybe throw a couple of my ghosts into the bargain?" Dietrich grinned, suddenly cheerful. As long as this world had free trade, he'd be fine. Especially once he'd laid his hands on a weapon which was a fast and proven way of solving any problem.

"No ghosts for me, thanks," Rich said, deadly serious. "You can keep them. Just remember what I've just told you."

"Okay, okay. Let me try. Don't you want to show me the Steiger first and teach me how to make the ammo?"

"As soon as I get your first memory, I'll make the gun. No ammo. Once I receive the second one, I'll show you how to make both ammo and new batteries."

"Being careful, are we? Never mind. It's a deal."

✳ ✳ ✳

"AND? How did you like it?"

"Don't ask," Space Forces Major Richard

Rowly winced with disgust. "At least the guy has some imagination, I have to give him that. What's with my neuromatrix?"

"It's stable. The memories are yours now. They integrated no problem. Can you imagine? We've just proved that it's possible to copy and paste neurograms! Don't you understand? Now it'll take days to train an expert in any field!"

"Not a healthy idea," the Major ordered a coffee and sat in a chair.

"Why? What's your problem?"

"The neuroimplant has too many mind traps. It's way too dangerous. We all have our own demons. Our job is to let them sleep undisturbed in the darkest corners of our minds."

"Did you have issues with that?"

"I did. But I can keep them in check... for the time being. But I don't think that Dietrich will survive his seven-day term."

"You feeling sorry for him?"

"Oh no, I'm not. It just got me thinking. Nobody's without sin. Implanting the whole Forces personnel with these things... I don't think it would be a good idea. Not a clever thing to do."

"We'll do that but not now, don't worry. First we're going to test the device in a computer game. The Chrystal Sphere, if you know what I mean. We already have an agreement with Infosystems. We'll have to block most of the implants' options for the time being. All we're going to leave is the full-immersion experience and the neurointerface. We also need to add a transmitting device which will allow us to read the neurograms and learn to work with them."

"Not exactly commendable, is it? This is a breach of privacy."

"I don't give a damn. Infosystems will keep their mouth shut. They're obliged to, for this kind of money. In the meantime, we're going to open a project of our own. Phantom Server. We'll recruit very selectively. We only need loners with no families or friends to worry about them, whether in real life or online."

"Why won't you try it yourself?" the Major snapped. Despite his mission's success, he felt like shit.

Colonel Jonathan Jyrd ignored his subordinate's quip. "I will when the time is right," he finally said. "I'd like you to do something else for me. There's a Corp technologist who works with us here, Jurgen's the name. I want you to keep an eye on him. I think he'll be good for us."

✳ ✳ ✳

DIETRICH WAS ANGRY, exhausted and depressed.

He didn't know how long it had been since Rich had left. Without the change of day and night you couldn't really tell. Hunger and thirst had ceased to be a problem; his memory, however, kept offering up nasty new surprises, materializing yet more ghosts of the past.

A life's worth of wickedness was catching up with him. Remembering his initial failure fighting the ghosts, he tried to ignore them even though it made things only worse.

The adaptable world hung on his every mood change, pelting him with icy wind and pouring rain. Aimlessly he staggered through the unknown as the puddles of water underfoot were being bound by ice.

He had nowhere to hide from the weather. His teeth were chattering. A crowd of phantoms trailed after him, some trying to catch up with him and look into his eyes, others attempting to say something that would remind him of themselves.

No amount of body pain could be compared to this agony of his tormented, trapped soul.

Before, he'd never given any thought to the idea of a soul. It had been easier to think it didn't exist. Having mastered getting rid of his weak pangs of conscience by shoving them deep into the recesses of his mind, he'd believed this to be the ultimate solution. In fact, he'd only been accumulating problems.

His Life bar kept shrinking, slowly but surely. He was already sick of all the system messages,

You're starving.

You're exhausted.

You're on the verge of a nervous breakdown.

New quest alert: Purgatory. It's time to reconcile with your past. In order to survive, you need to embrace your memories.

Dietrich stopped and looked behind him. The disorderly crowd of his mortal sins scared him witless. Even if he managed to last the required seven days, what kind of person would he leave this place?

A drooling idiot with a shaking head? Would he be able to live as if nothing had happened, ignoring the consequences of his deeds?

They'd called it a deal! They'd surely known he wouldn't survive it!

A new surge of fury flooded his thoughts. To hell with their quests! There was no way he reconciled with this bunch of monsters! He should forget them, as simple as that. Amnesia sufferers could do it, couldn't they? They just started a new life from scratch. Sounded all right to him!

His finger touched the gun's yielding trigger.

There was only one way to check if he was right.

He raised his hand and fired. Again. And

again.

Time to purge my memory!

Each flash echoed with pain. His vision darkened. Still, he continued firing at the crowd, knowing he couldn't miss.

✳ ✳ ✳

HE FAINTED several times, regaining consciousness only to continue exterminating the unwanted memories. Surprised, he concentrated on the new emptiness taking root in his heart. Each new shot came easier than the one before it.

He got used to the pain. The weather improved somewhat. Gradually the wind died down.

There was very little of him left, literally. Having lost most of his life's experience, Dietrich had turned into somebody else: someone angry and obstinate. The only thing he still remembered was his name.

By now, he didn't differ much from the ghosts that used to surround him. His body had turned translucent and ephemeral, distorted by surges of interference. His face was flattening, losing its individual features as it turned into a crude grotesque mask.

Finally, it too disappeared.

Dozens of people witnessed his loss of

identity.

"Gone," Colonel Jyrd commented. "Dead."

"His physical body is still alive," Jurgen pointed out.

"His physical body is only a mantle. You can switch off the life support systems now. I'll sign the paperwork. The convict volunteer didn't survive the tests performed with his written consent. End of story. Block the neuroimplant's Absolute Memory function until further notice. That's it, let's do it!!"

THE TESTING GROUNDS were divided into separate locations controlled by reliable secure servers. This included the neurocomputers providing the automatic neuromatrix support.

Months turned into years as new technologies advanced, introducing new settings. Sets of tests followed non-stop. New models of in-game objects were being downloaded in order to be fine-tuned and consequently deleted.

The world of the Crystal Sphere was growing popular. Quite a few players received new devices which offered a 100% authenticity of their gaming experience. Rumors began to circulate about the mysterious Phantom Server: a game of the future based exclusively on neurotechnologies. Still, no one really knew its release date.

The introduction of neuroimplants had allowed many of the Infosystems workers to relocate online, working, living and even sleeping in cyber space.

* * *

THERE WAS VERY LITTLE of him left. Only a few neurograms were still held together by his last and only memory: Dietrich still remembered his own name. That was the only thing that kept him from complete disintegration.

He'd become the rustle of the wind; a ripple in the fabric of reality; a barely visible haze floating in the air. A faint shadow that couldn't even trigger the scanners' sensors.

Sometimes as he watched humans, he experienced a vague longing: a craving born of desperation. He wanted to own their emotions; to reap their experiences. In moments like those he felt strangely confident that he could lay his hands on their neurograms — provided he was just a little bit stronger.

The craving kept growing, the desire to reap what he hadn't sown thwarted by his own impotence. He was too weak to attack — so he didn't, shrinking into the shadows whenever humans approached.

It all changed overnight. As he watched a

well-equipped group of corporate workers test out a new batch of mobs about to be introduced into the Crystal Sphere, he witnessed a man die.

One of the team members failed to dodge an ugly monster's blow. It had happened before. Normally, it ended with some quality cussing and the hapless player's respawn.

Not today, though.

Enveloped in a pale glow, the identity of the unfortunate worker began to disintegrate into separate neurograms. Back in the real world his physical body had died, unable to survive the agonizing pain.

Dietrich didn't know that. Instinctively he darted forward, trying to imbibe a few of the melting sparks of light.

He grew somewhat. It hadn't quenched his craving, though. He needed more.

The worker's few disjointed memories contained a basic weapons skill.

This incident showed him the way. He knew that sooner or later he'd be lucky enough to come across another such accident, enabling him to imbibe a few more drops of another person's identity.

One of these days he'd have enough neurograms to attack and take what was rightfully his.

Having completed their testing, the

Corporation workers finally left.

He stood alone in the deserted location. Barely visible, helpless and pathetic. The first fruit of the looming digital Apocalypse. His craving grew stronger.

He was now ready to reap.

MAY 2016

TRANSLATED FROM RUSSIAN BY IRENE WOODHEAD AND NEIL P. MAYHEW

Throne World

(From the Life of Crown Princesses)

A tale from *Perimeter Defense* series

by Michael Atamanov

The Arites are an intelligent, nonhumanoid, non-protein-based life form. Their homeworld is thought to be a planet in the Arite star system, which is located in the Swarm cluster, though they can also be found in all neighboring star systems. The Arites possess a surprising ability. They can perfectly imitate the physical form, communication patterns and behavior of any creature they've had contact with. In their subsequent interactions with other intelligent life forms, they also learned to detect and bypass electronic security systems. The Arites were discovered around two hundred years ago by the Iseyek (a symbiotic federation of intelligent insectoid races commonly known as the Swarm) and were declared dangerous parasites. This determination would lead to a two-hundred-year war between the groups. However, the Iseyek were never able to fully exterminate the Arites and, finally, with Human mediation, a historic peace treaty was signed, which made the Arites members of the Swarm.

(from an online encyclopedia article)

**Imperial Core. Throne World.
An elite preparatory school for children
of the upper Imperial aristocracy.
Girls' dormitory wing.**

W HY DO CROWN PRINCESSES have to bring so much stuff with them? I stared in horror at the mountain of suitcases and boxes my friends and I had brought back to school after summer vacation. Back at home, there were servants to carry our bags and suitcases, but here that wasn't possible – servants weren't allowed at our elite school. What a pity...

I clicked open the lock of the nearest huge suitcase and looked glumly at the neatly folded packets of clothing. Were these even my things? Not so long ago, we were all looking through a catalogue together, and my friend Crown Princess Natalie came up with the idea for us all to buy the exact same bags to bring back to school. Back then, it seemed like such a cool plan. But now, with all our baggage piled up in the entryway, we realized just what a bad choice we made. We played rock paper scissors to decide who would have to dig their bags out of the towering pile first. And I lost. My friends were now off in the next room watching cartoons, leaving me alone to break first ground in the heaps of luggage. I picked right on the first try, though. I looked at one of the transparent packets inside the open suitcase, and saw the neatly packaged souvenirs I'd been given by loyal insects in Dekeye, the Swarm capital.

I opened my wardrobe, and froze for some time, staring at my reflection in the big mirror on its inner door. A pretty, healthy girl was looking back at me with big gray-green eyes and long hair dyed an alternating pattern of emerald-green and pink just like in all the teenage fashion articles. I held my gaze on the image for a few seconds, and an interactive guide popped up before my eyes:

> **Likanna royl Georg ton Mesfelle-Unatari, Crown Princess of the Empire, ruler of the Yal star system**
> **Age: 13**
> **Race: Human**
> **Gender: Female**
> **Class: Aristocrat**
> **Achievements: Swarm Princess**
> **Fame: +8**
> **Standing: +2**

My fame in the Empire had grown sharply in the last few months. It was pretty awesome! I'd become the bona fide ruler of the Yal system, which had a population of eleven billion nonhumanoids. And beyond that, I was now first in line to the throne of the sprawling Unatari State, which consisted of nearly one hundred inhabitable star systems. Recently my father, the ruler of Unatari, told me I was now one of the most desired brides in the Universe, and soon, there would be a line of bachelors asking for my hand stretching from my palace gates to the very horizon. And my dad proved to be right. Despite my young age, I already had plenty of admirers. I constantly received personal messages from aristocrats I didn't know suggesting we get acquainted. But on my father's advice, I simply ignored them. I already knew my worth and understood that the true upper crust of the Great Imperial Houses wouldn't make such crude overtures.

My thoughts were interrupted by a shout from my friends:

"Lika! You have to come over here! Your dad's about to give a speech on the news!"

I set the suitcase aside, its contents already hung up in the wardrobe, and bolted into the common room. My friends, the Crown Princesses Joan and Natalie, scooted over, making me a place to sit on the small couch in front of the huge screen on the wall.

And just then, my father appeared – Crown Prince Georg royl Inoky ton Mesfelle, the ruler of the interstellar Unatari State and one of the greatest fleet commanders of the modern era. From the screen, a fifty-year-old slightly chubby man with a visible flock of gray in his dark mane was looking down sternly at the viewers. My father's right cheek was crossed from one brow to the opposite lip by a jagged scar he'd gotten in the explosion of his flagship, the heavy assault cruiser *Joan the Fatty* during one of his innumerable battles with the Aliens.

I had suggested that he get it looked at by a cosmetic surgeon many times. They'd have been able to get rid of that repugnant disfiguration. But Georg refused. He said the old wound reminded him of his grandiose victory in the Aysar Cluster and made him look more manly. To my eye, it was a bit much. Everyone in the Empire already knew my father as a hero of that war, and the only thing he needed to emphasize that was his dark blue fleet commander uniform with gold epaulets.

> ***Georg royl Inoky ton Mesfelle, Crown Prince of the Empire, Ruler of the Unatari State, Swarm Five-Star-Admiral***
> ***Age: 49***
> ***Race: Human***
> ***Gender: Male***
> ***Class: Aristocrat/Mystic***
> ***Relation to you: Your father***
> ***Achievements: Elder Chameleon Female, Discovered Arites, Got through***

Alien Blockade, Researcher of the Unknown, Imperial Land Grabber, Ex-Fleet Commander for Sector Eight, Malingerer, Respected by the Swarm, Dekeye Champion of No Rules Fighting, Defender of Humanity, Master of the Hive, Favorite's Iseyek Mating Dance.

Fame: +68

Standing: +21

Presumed personal opinion of you: +100 (completely trusting)

Yes, my father's achievement list was an impressive, dramatic retelling of his tumultuous life story.

Just after he started his speech, my friends and I started gaping in surprise, unable to believe what we were hearing. It was pretty shocking stuff – my father, in no uncertain terms, was accusing Emperor August of a treacherous attack on an Unatari diplomatic mission, the murder of his bodyguards, and also an attempt on his very life, as well as that of his cousin Duchess Katerina royl Unatari.

My father gave Emperor August exactly one day to issue an official apology and pay five billion in compensation for the destruction of his personal yacht, and the murder of his bodyguards and crew members. If not, the ruler of Unatari promised to declare independence from the Empire and was threatening to give an order to destroy all military divisions and fleets in Unatari space still loyal to Emperor August. And it was all said in language far too biting to be used in typical diplomatic correspondence. In fact, "bearded nutjob" and "old goat" were the most appropriate names my father called the Emperor.

The emergency news broadcast came to an end, and the cartoon my friends had been watching came back on. But we were just sitting in silence, unable to come back to our senses.

My father had an extremely mixed reputation. There were plenty of moments from his biography that even made me, his doting daughter, blush in embarrassment. All three of Crown Prince Georg's children had different mothers for example, and there was also the unfortunate fact that his retinue contained Bionica, a sex robot. It was the subject of far too many jokes for my liking. The Orange House accused my father of rebellion and upending their legal authority, illegally occupying Perimeter Sectors Eight and Nine, assassinating political opponents, and forcing people to resign from power with threats of violence. But at that, no one, not even his most fervent foes could deny my father's impressive abilities as a fleet commander and diplomat, as well as his leading role in liberating star systems from Alien control.

Some adored my father and deified him. Others feared and hated him. But both groups could be sure that Crown Prince Georg royl Inoky ton Mesfelle didn't make idle threats! I didn't doubt for a second that my father really would give an order to destroy millions of Imperial soldiers if he didn't get what he was demanding from the Emperor. And I knew that no potential consequences could stop him.

"Your father has totally lost it!" said my best friend, the Purple House princess, Joan royl Reyekh. And in her voice, I could hear unhidden horror. "Your father's military victories have gone to his head and he has completely lost his link with reality! He clearly didn't think this through! I mean, making an ultimatum to the ruler of the Empire himself? He can't possibly think seriously that Emperor August is going to back down, right?"

"Well, I doubt he just made the ultimatum off the cuff," replied Crown Princess Natalie royl Cruz. A former Blue House Princess, she was now a subject of the Unatari State. "Likanna's father is the greatest military strategist of modern times, and he has a very strong space fleet under his command. He would never make such drastic accusations if he hadn't considered all the possible consequences. In the end, Crown Prince Georg decided to make this accusatory speech, so that must mean he thinks he can win."

"That sounds right," I agreed with her. "But this looks pretty bad for me and you. We are both Unatari subjects, and the Emperor may see us as perspective hostages for trading with my father."

Natalie nodded in silence, but Crown Princess Joan then grew sincerely indignant:

"What on earth are you talking about, Lika?! All Imperial Crown Princesses are absolutely untouchable, no matter what Great House they belong to! August wouldn't dare lay a finger on you!"

I chuckled back sadly:

"I would also like to believe in justice and the sanctity of the law. But the Emperor did dare to shoot the Unatari delegation to the Throne World even though all diplomats are also supposed to be untouchable. And he tried to kill my father, even though Crown Prince Georg royl Inoky is also theoretically untouchable. Basically, I say let's wait and see..."

[Mission received: Obtain a personal meeting with the Emperor]

[Mission received: Obtain the Emperor's agreement to the ultimatum]

The messages caught me off guard. I even shuddered. Then I read the text and shuddered again. Just look at that! How was I even supposed to accomplish that?! Crown Princess Natalie raised her gaze to meet mine, letting me know she had also received these missions. Crown Princess Joan, though, for whom these events were of little relevance, remained calm and even went back to watching the cartoon.

I gestured with my eyes to Natalie in the direction of the neighboring room. There we could speak alone, not worrying about who could hear us. She understood me, and stood up.

"There is a camera and microphone in the wall over your bed," Natalie whispered to me barely audibly as soon as we'd left the room and closed the door.

"Yes, I noticed," I confirmed. "These perverts are sneaking peeks at little girls!"

We both exchanged glances and cracked up laughing. Then Natalie put on a serious expression and stated:

"Lika, I'm afraid the Emperor won't try to meet with us. It seems quite likely to me that August doesn't even know we're on the Throne World. And what's more, I'm pretty sure the Emperor won't try to take you and I hostage. It would cause too much stink. Taking two Crown Princesses against their will would be a big story."

"That means we'll have to make it happen then," I chuckled and cocked my eye at her. "We need to make such a loud statement that the Throne World news channels will talk about nothing but you and me. That way, August will have to notice us."

My friend nodded in understanding. A minute later, Crown Princess Natalie was drawing up a press release to send off to the largest Throne World news agencies, telling them to send reporters to the gates of our preparatory school and film the scandalous, illegal arrest of two underage Crown Princesses. I then, from the hacked account of our school's administration, made false reports to the Throne World Security Service about kidnapping threats against two Imperial Crown Princesses and demanded they be provided armed guards and transport to a safe location.

I HELD A WOEFUL EXPRESSION on my face with all my might, trying my best not to crack up. Our plan had its intended effect. It actually turned out better than we were expecting. In just one hour's time, there was a whole host of reporters gathered before the gates of our prep school, camera operators in tow. Alongside them was a separate crowd of curious onlookers who greeted the arriving convoy with an angry roar. The huge number of armed Throne World Security Service personnel that came out of the ships grimaced when they saw the giant crowd of people, but they continued to determinedly muscle their way through the crowd to their shuttle.

Before taking a seat in the armor-plated Security Service shuttle, I turned to the crowd and waved my hand good-naturedly. The people below gave an enthusiastic shout in response.

Global fame increase. Current value +9

Global standing increase. Current value +3

Geez! I guess it was playing out perfectly! The Security Service officer obligingly threw open the shuttle doors before me and let me inside. Crown Princess Natalie was already there. The door closed on its own, leaving the two of us alone in the small but comfortable vehicle.

"There's a video camera over the viewport," she mouthed to me.

"As soon as we get off the ground, block it. We'll leave quietly and blend in with the crowd," I whispered back as quietly as possible.

A minute later, Natalie and I were already standing on a park path, hidden from the crowd behind a thicket of vegetation. We slinked away from the guards, and now we were observing the armored vehicle, its engines humming in exertion as they gained altitude. It turned toward the setting sun, which was orange in this system. The crowd shouted a bit more after the retreating shuttle and was already beginning to disperse when suddenly... four sleek atmospheric-near-space interceptors dove out of the clouds and launched a barrage of rockets at the shuttle! Leaving a clear white trail in the air, the homing rockets darted toward the vehicle for a few seconds, as it attempted an awkward dodge maneuver.

Boom!!!

In the evening sky, there bloomed a huge bright flower. After that, fragments of the armored aircraft poured down on us. Natalie and I were standing, shivering, and staring wide-eyed at the smoky cloud where the shuttle had once been as we listened to the hysterical screams of the crowd. Natalie snapped out of the trance before I did:

"Holy crap! We were just trying to attract attention. But now, it looks like someone was really trying to kill us! Two Imperial Crown

Princesses!"

The story really had taken a surprising and (why hide it?) extremely unpleasant turn. This was an attempt on our lives and, what's more, it was done before the eyes of thousands of people which clearly played into our hand.

"Natalie, I think we should go away for a half hour so all the news channels will say that we died. I bet the news will reach the Emperor by then and, when we appear alive and well, August will be told immediately."

And that was what we did, simply walking down the park paths away from the scene of the crime. Eventually, we took a seat on a bench in a quiet, desolate area. We were both watching the news on our palmtops. And though the central Throne World channels were keeping mum, all the other channels had our story front and center. There were many versions being told, but the majority of commentators linked the attack with the ultimatum given to the Emperor a few hours earlier.

Finally, after about an hour, the Emperor's secretariat issued an official press release calling the alleged attempt on two Imperial Crown Princesses mere rumors, and probably intentional disinformation. According to the Throne World's official story, what really happened was that some as-of-yet-unknown criminal structures attempted to hijack a police shuttle, which caused the aircraft to be shot down. There were five corpses found in the wreckage, and all of them belonged to adult males. There were no female bodies there, and certainly no children.

Nevertheless, the Emperor's press secretary was not able to answer a direct question from a journalist asking where Crown Princesses Likanna royl Unatari and Natali royl Unatari were currently. He only assured everyone that the location of the two royal children would be discovered very, very soon.

"It seems like now is the best time to go public," my friend suggested.

"Yes, I agree. It's time we showed ourselves, now that the Emperor's secretariat has decided to start searching for us."

We walked unhurriedly to the end of the long shady path and purposely passed by a camera installed near a monument, knowing full well that it was detecting the faces of all passersby and cross-referencing that with a central database. A few minutes later, a police patrol came down the path. A young woman in a severe criminal-police uniform pressed her palm to her helmet in a sign of greeting:

"Crown Princesses Natalie and Likanna I presume? Would your Highnesses please follow me to the police station?"

Natalie and I exchanged glances. My friend twisted her face up and said in dismay:

"And what if we don't want to? You cannot force us to go against our will."

"Of course not. We never even thought of forcing you," said the second police officer, a buff man with graying hair. It's just that we've been searching for you two for a while, and we want to accompany you to a safe location."

"You know, I remember a time when we were free to just go on a walk without intrusive round-the-clock observation..." I mumbled for appearances, but then all the same agreed to follow the police. Natalie didn't argue either.

✳ ✳ ✳

THE POLICE DIVISION HEAD was very happy and even let us hang out in his personal office while they talked over the issue of what to do with us "somewhere up the ranks." They were, of course, elated to have found us two Crown Princesses alive and well. As Natalie and I, sitting on big spinning leather chairs, drank sparkling water and stress-ate some pastries, a reporter asked us tricky questions. It was unclear how he'd gotten access to the police building, though. First of all, he wanted to know why we hadn't flown away in the armored vehicle sent to us by the Throne World Security Service. As I chomped down a cream-filled pastry, I put on my best look of ambivalence and answered:

"Before bringing us through the crowd of journalists, one of the Security Service officers warned us that it was all just for appearances, to throw off the bad guys and that we wouldn't actually be going anywhere. So, we were led into the shuttle in full view, then secretly taken out the other side. A group of officers blocked us with their backs, and we walked behind some thick bushes and waited there for a while. But then the shuttle blew up, and they all forgot about us. After that, we decided to leave that boring place and just go for a walk."

"But your Highness, that was very bad judgment!" the reporter gaped. "Whoever organized the attack on the vehicle could have kidnapped you in the park when you were both unguarded!"

"Yeah, well, what were they gonna do? I mean, we're Imperial Crown Princesses and so we're absolutely untouchable..." the end of my phrase was drowned out by a worrying clanging sound coming from down the hall.

All three of us exchanged surprised glances, not understanding what was going on. A few seconds later, from behind the closed door, we heard gunfire and angry shouting. The reporter who'd been questioning us (or maybe it wasn't a reporter at all, based on the short-barreled laser rifle and light armored vest he took out of his briefcase) ordered Natalie and I to go away from the door and sit in the corner of the room. He, clearly having a lot of experience, assembled his weapon and very nearly shot when the office door opened abruptly. But it was the head of the police division. He was wounded and holding his lifeless, bloody left arm in his right hand.

"It's pretty rough out there!" he blurted out, hurriedly locking the massive door behind him. "The whole first floor and hallway of the second have been captured by assault troops in heavy armored suits. Based on their emblems, they're from a nearby military outpost. Why they attacked, I have no idea. My lieutenant tried to find out the reason for the invasion, but they didn't listen to him, just shot him full of holes. Basically, they're shooting everyone. Even people who surrender, or ones who never had weapons to begin with."

"What are they armed with?" inquired the false reporter, already having managed to strap into his armored vest and shoving extra clips and grenades into his pockets.

"The attackers have high-speed plasma

rifles, cluster grenade launchers and infantry combat resonators."

"Not exactly the weaponry you'd bring to an assault, if you wanted to capture anybody alive..." our protector said gloomily, and the police head nodded back without a word.

"Is the video camera still live? Can anyone not in the building see what it's filming?" asked Natalie. The questions sounded inappropriately chipper in my friend's sonorous feminine voice, given the terrifying situation.

Both men turned and stared at Natalie and me. The reporter looked at the device attached to his tripod and confirmed it was transmitting.

"Alrighty then!" Natalie exclaimed, growing joyful and turning to the camera. "I, Crown Princess Natalie royl Cruz ton Unatari, officially declare that I will be outside the doors of my prep school in two hours. And I demand that Emperor August royl Akad provide for my safety which he, as the ruler of the Empire, must provide to all upper aristocrats. My friend, Crown Princess Likanna royl Georg ton Unatari-Mesfelle will be there too, and she also needs protection. And now," my friend turned to our defenders, "I ask you to turn off all the recording equipment. Lika and I are going to escape this besieged police station and do not want to leave any clues about how we got out or where we went."

The "reporter" was too surprised and intrigued by the little girl's words to argue. Just after he turned off his camera, my friend pointed to a small ventilation shaft in the wall and shouted: "In there!"

The police head looked where she pointed and hurried to object:

"It's no use, your Highness! The ventilation shaft back there is too narrow. A person would never be ab..." he said, stopping mid-word with his mouth hanging wide open, as Natalie and I just went in. Without even taking off the grate.

THEY WERE OBVIOUSLY waiting for us to show up. The whole area around our prep school was lit up with bright spotlights, surrounded by soldiers and armored vehicles, and covered with a defensive force field. In the twilight sky, there were dozens of recon drones hovering, and combat aircraft patrolling. The armed soldiers gave way, letting Natalie and I through. Their ranks closed behind us just as swiftly, leaving the many gathered journalists and curious onlookers blocked off.

Right at the very gates of the prep school, arms crossed behind his back, there was a gray-haired medium-height man standing in a luxurious bright-red robe. In his silvery ashen hair I could clearly make out the golden band of a crown. I read his information:

Julius royl August ton Akad, Duke of the Empire
   Age: 189
   Race: Human
   Gender: Male
   Class: Aristocrat/Artist
   Relation to you: Your great uncle
   Achievements: Primus inter Pares, Collector, Gained respect, Maecenate.
   Fame: +99
   Standing: +108
   Presumed personal relationship: Unknown

That's what I'm talking about! The man waiting for Natalie and I turned out to be the Emperor's own oldest son, first in line to the throne and one of the most influential people in the whole Universe! I was immediately reassured. I knew I could trust this man. Duke Julius wouldn't attack two young Princesses no matter what. Doing that could sully his flawless reputation as an honest and noble man, which he had spent practically two centuries to earn. In accordance with courtly etiquette, Crown

Princess Natalie royl Cruz and I stopped three steps from the senior aristocrat and gave delicate bows. We managed to do it in unison and gracefully. The Duke smiled in approval.

"So here are the little Princesses who've got the whole Empire so worked up, while they flit about walking through parks and disappearing. Get into the shuttle, girls. The Emperor would like to see you in the Silver Palace for a personal conversation."

We bowed politely to Duke Julius once again and got on board his luxuriant shuttle. It was a true flying palace, decked out in gold, platinum and gemstones. The pictures on the walls were from famous artists, and the viewports were carved of artificial sapphire crystals. I had only ever seen such luxury before on *Queen of Sin*, my father's personal yacht.

No less than ten aircraft of various types accompanied our take-off, and two of them followed us the whole way, constantly maintaining a defensive shield around the Duke's shuttle. Only when the vehicle had gained altitude and speed did the escorts fall back.

"Now, our cover is coming from space," Julius said, having noticed my interest. "We are being tracked by laser turrets from the Throne World's orbital citadel. They can destroy any potential danger in an instant. They will destroy any aircraft that comes within a certain distance of us, as a matter of fact. The whole area we're flying through right now is subject to a no-fly zone. No one other than our shuttle is allowed to be up here. Yes, they are harsh measures, but after the series of strange events that happened today, my father didn't want to leave anything up to chance."

"Have you found out who is behind all these shadowy attacks?" I asked, not especially counting on an answer, as the information was probably top secret.

But Duke Julius answered nonetheless, and didn't even hide the truth:

"Yes, the crews of the interceptors have already been arrested, as well as the whole assault group that attacked the police station. What made it so strange was that they didn't even resist the arrest. They all claimed they were carrying out direct orders from the Emperor. Checks by the best psionics and with the most advanced lie detectors have confirmed that the soldiers were not lying, either. They all truly believe the illegal orders came directly from my father. And that is the weirdest part. Someone has been doing a very skillful imitation of the Emperor. His standing has fallen sharply after all these scandals. My father didn't like that one bit, and that is the very reason he wanted to get to the bottom of all this himself. By the way, we've arrived. There is the Silver Palace in all its glory."

I looked out the viewport. It was quite a sight to see. In the anthracite blackness of the night sky, the towers of the palace shimmered like silver needles, reflecting the glow of the spotlights at their base. Despite the colossal size of the Emperor's official residence, from the bird's eye view we now had, the palace seemed like a toy based on an ancient children's fable. The image was spoiled only by the flickering of the defensive shield that covered the building's half-kilometer-high spires in a huge dome. I couldn't resist making a negative comment on the force field.

"What can you do? These are tough times. The bloody war with the Aliens has been going on for three years now. The Red House just fell to their onslaught. The Empire lost two Perimeter Sectors. And also, all our sources say the Antagonists will invade any day now. This just adds to that. The Swarm, the traditional rival of humanity, has grown significantly stronger in a very short time. And your father, Crown Prince Georg royl Inoky ton Mesfelle played a significant part in that. Some of the Crown Prince's actions are hard to look on as anything other than extremely bad judgment that goes so far as to pose a threat to humanity. I mean, why did he have to help the Swarm fight the Aliens?! He could have let our rivals get weaker and destroy one another! Instead, he armed our potential enemies and gave them modern military technology. That goes far beyond the bounds of rationality and borders on treason!"

I shot up from my seat, looked the old man right in the eyes and said with determination:

"Duke Julius, it is not for you to judge my father's actions! Crown Prince Georg understands the structure of the Swarm better than anyone else. He's also very knowledgeable on the psychology of the Iseyek race. Their hundreds of billions of intelligent insects are not an enemy to humanity, but a powerful tool in interstellar politics, which can and must be used. Destroying the Swarm by force was absolutely impossible. Fifty years of bloody war against them should have taught you that, Duke. After all, you were a witness to those dark times. But then, achieving the respect and trust of the insects, making them allies, and eventually even coming to rule the Swarm itself is the very path humanity should be on!"

The old man chuckled, easily bearing my gaze and hateful speech.

Duke Julius' opinion of you has improved. Current opinion: +15 (warm)

Global standing increase. Current value +4

"Crown Princess Likanna, your character is very much like that of your father. You are both decisive and strangely self-assured. You both also have a total disregard for the opinions of all others. But your point of view is not the only one. The Swarm has long been a threat to the Empire, due to its economic and military might. But the Iseyek used to be quite forthright and predictable. Now though, with your father at their head, the threat has grown by many times as the insects have a human ruler. And he is an unprincipled unpredictable ruler, who is cruel and cunning. My father could not make peace with that threat, and that is the only explanation for today's attack on the Unatari embassy. Princess, it has been a great pleasure to speak with you. You are wise beyond your young years. But now, we have arrived. Crown Princess Natalie, Crown Princess Likanna, I ask you to follow me. The ruler of the Empire awaits you."

NOT SO LONG AGO, I'd had the thought that there were a lot of soldiers waiting for us near the gates of our prep school. But my perspective was different now. The number of soldiers there wasn't really so great. The huge crowd now before the Silver Palace truly deserved the descriptor. All the hallways, passageways and stairwells were jammed with armed soldiers. We walked through a succession of rooms and stopped before a set of elevated carved doors. The guards broke ranks and opened them, letting the Duke and us into the poorly lit room.

[Mission completed: Obtain a personal meeting with the Emperor]

"Search them!" a tall harrier-gray old man standing behind us ordered without even turning.

"But how can we, father? They are Crown Princesses, after all! It is not accepted practice!" Our escort flared up, but all the same stepped aside, letting the Emperor's bodyguards through.

"The ruler of Unatari, Crown Prince Georg, brought a hidden camera with him into a secret meeting today and broadcast it to the whole galaxy. So, I have a pretty good idea of where 'accepted practice' gets you! The girls will survive the search. Nothing more will be done to them."

A silent bodyguard approached me and ran a complex detector over my body, searching for metal, electronics or explosives. Without even asking my permission, he took my palmtop out of my pants pocket, and also unlatched my gold necklace and silently stripped me of it. The search of my friend Crown Princess Natalie also didn't last long.

"All clean. No contraband," the guard sounded off and walked away from us, carrying the confiscated items away on a small round tray.

Only after that did the old man at the window stop contemplating and have the grace to turn around.

> *August royl Toll ton Akad, Emperor*
> *Age: 340 years*
> *Race: Human*
> *Gender: Male*
> *Relation to you: Your great great uncle*
> *Class: Aristocrat*
> *Achievements: (see Attachment)*
> *Fame: +99*
> *Standing: + 234*
> *Presumed personal opinion of you: Unknown*

Crown Princess Natalie and I greeted the ruler of the Empire with the deepest of bows, in full accordance with noble etiquette, but the old man didn't react in any way. Instead, he gave a groan and flopped down heavily in a deep armchair then demanded from his guards in a grumbling, grating voice:

"Close the doors and turn on the electronics suppression system. I've had quite enough unpleasant surprises for one day."

A few seconds later, Natalie mouthed to me:

"All the cameras have been turned off!"

"Yep. An electromagnetic field just came on, too. This room is totally cut off from the rest of the world now," I whispered back.

And though I was basically speaking silently, the Emperor still managed to overhear something and got on guard:

"What are you whispering about over there? Huh? Please repeat it out loud for everyone."

I looked at my friend and she nodded in agreement. Then I straightened up and said in a calm, self-assured voice:

"Very well. My friend and I were discussing the fact that the room is isolated, the cameras have been turned off, and no one from outside will hear or see what happens here. Are you not afraid to be left alone with us, your Imperial Majesty? I mean, after your treacherous attack on my father's delegation?"

The Emperor clearly was not expecting such words and lost his place. He looked at his son Julius, then the four guards in the room and gave an exhausted laugh:

"I think my people will be able to handle two little Princesses just fine. And your father himself was in the wrong today. The Swarm is no mere plaything! Crown Prince Georg does not understand that intelligent insects are dangerous! They need to be weakened or destroyed while we still have the chance!"

"We do not have that chance, and never did!" shouted Crown Princess Natalie. "The insects are prolific and hard working. They restore any losses very quickly both in number and military technology. That is why the biggest mistake humanity could make would be to begin measuring itself against the Swarm in brute force. Crown Prince Georg royl Inoky understood that, which is why he took a different path. He earned the trust of the insects, became ruler of the Swarm and thus gave humanity a powerful force that can be controlled."

"Crown Prince Georg and his Unatari State are far from all of humanity. And Georg is a naive fool, as he allowed the insects to wrap him around their collective finger!" Emperor August replied sharply, almost beginning to scream. "The Swarm needs an experienced fleet commander to lead their starship armadas against humanity, and they found it in Likanna's father. And as soon as the necessity for a human ruler passes, the insects will rid themselves of him. They will simply devour him, along with the rest of humanity."

I just shook my head in reproach:

"Your Imperial Majesty, you have a very poor understanding of the Iseyek mindset! Think about an anthill or a bee hive. Would the drones living and working in it ever take up opposition against their Queen, or harm her in any way? No, that would be impossible. It is the same with the Iseyek. As soon as Crown Prince Georg royl Inoky ton Mesfelle became ruler of the Swarm, all hundreds of billions of intelligent insects became unwaveringly loyal to him. Obeying the Master of the Swarm is embedded in the Iseyek gene code. None of the insects will even think to do harm to the Master of the Swarm. And at that, any Iseyek would give their life for him without a second thought."

It was not easy to convince the Emperor we were right. He was being stubborn.

"Georg will not live forever. A few decades or even centuries will pass, but one day he will be no more. And then, all the crushing might of the Swarm will cease to be under humanity's control! It will only get stronger!"

I shrugged my shoulders ambiguously:

"Who knows what will happen in such a distant future? I think Crown Prince Georg will take measures to ensure that control of the Swarm will remain with his children. Now, though, the insects are absolutely fine with the situation; they have a talented ruler who takes good care of them. The Swarm has absolutely no need for the imminent war between the Unatari State and the rest of the Empire. That is why I return back to my initial question. Emperor, are you not afraid to be left alone with us?"

August grew noticeably on edge and inquired cautiously:

"What are you implying, Likanna?"

"Simply that the Swarm is not only the praying-mantis Alpha Iseyek soldiers, hardworking Beta Iseyek centipedes and wise overgrown pill-bug Gamma Iseyek. The Swarm also includes the Arite Iseyek, who are capable of taking any appearance. Emperor, think about what happened today. Crown Princess Natalie and I managed to escape a shuttle in mid-flight, then we left a surrounded building unnoticed. And before all this, did it seriously not occur to you that Crown Prince Georg is not so thoughtless as to send his beloved daughter to the Throne World? Did you not think he might foresee the attempt on his life, or the way this might play out?"

The old man's lips started quivering. His teeth were chattering lightly.

"Likanna, so you are... an Arite?" August barely squeezed out.

I took the intermediary form of a little white cloud, then a second later chose the appearance of the old man himself. Then my one-for-one copy of Emperor August took its place standing next to the original. A second later, Natalie completed the same transformation, and a third Emperor joined our rank. August turned to his bodyguards, perplexed. But, in the place the sullen soldiers had been standing, there were now another four Emperors.

"And now, if you please, I'll try something more original," Duke Julius laughed, changing form to my roommate, Crown Princess Joan royl Reyekh. "I've been Emperor August more than enough for one day. It was I that gave the orders to the soldiers and assigned the divisions to patrol the Silver Palace."

"Where... then is my... oldest son?" the old man spoke out sparsely through quivering lips.

"Where do you think he is at this hour?" Crown Princess Joan asked, surprised. "I'm sure Duke Julius is sleeping in his summer residence. At his age, and with his weak health, keeping a regular schedule is very important. But now, I suggest we return to the previous topic of conversation. The Swarm has no need whatsoever for a war between the Unatari State and the Empire, so we are firmly intent on avoiding it. Your Imperial Majesty, you must agree to the conditions set by Crown Prince Georg, beg his official forgiveness and pay him the requested compensation. After that, we will leave your palace without doing any harm to you or any others. But if you do not agree, someone else will do it for you," said Joan royl Reyekh, leading her hand over the hall and pointing to the six other identical copies of August. "But in that case, you can easily understand that we will no longer have any need for the original. The choice is yours."

The old man folded his quivering hands together on his chest and paced through the room. Then he stopped and asked:

"It is important for me to know, was all this," the Emperor pointed at his many doubles, "organized by my grandnephew Georg?"

"No, we didn't bother the Master of the Swarm with such small details. This was completely the initiative of the Swarm. As a matter of fact, this is our gift to our new ruler and, at the same time, a demonstration of our abilities. The real Crown Princesses Likanna, Natalie and Joan are also in no way aware of the goings-on and, I suppose, are very surprised at the strange news from the Throne World and the standing and global-fame change messages they keep getting. But, I think they will not be too offended by the fact that we increased their visibility and popularity."

Emperor August stopped decisively in the center of the room and turned sharply:

"My advisers must have been giving me unreliable information on the Swarm for many years. They describe the Iseyek as predictable and extremely bloodthirsty. But now I see that is not at all the case. Many heads in the Imperial Joint Chiefs will fly for this mistake. It seems that, even after so many years, humanity knows precious little about its neighbors. Alright, I'll officially beg forgiveness from Georg and pay him the five billion. But on the condition that the events in this room will not be made known to a wider audience, and all Arites immediately leave my palace."

"That is quite alright with us," I answered for all of them, again taking the appearance of Crown Princess Likanna.

[Mission completed: Obtain the Emperor's agreement to the ultimatum]

Rank in hierarchy increased. You are now a Member of the Arite Council.

"WANNA GO BACK to prep school?" Crown Princess Natalie asked, already flying over the night ocean in the Duke's shuttle.

"No, it would take us at least two days just to pack those bags again," I reminded them, shivering unwillingly from the memory. "Better to just order the baggage sent back to Unatari. Let the servants handle it."

"I also see no point in flying back to prep school," Joan confirmed. "Let's bring Duke Julius's plane back to its place and run off on new missions. Crown Prince Georg always has lots of jobs for the Arites. Now that he's our ruler, I suspect we'll have quite a lot to do. Were you seriously considering going to study among these aristocratic brats instead of spying for the Unatari State?"

We cracked up laughing, then kept quiet for a bit. Joan broke the silence:

"It's nice being a Human. I like it. I even think from time to time that I should take the form of some average person forever and just live like the rest of them. Perhaps the Arites are making the wrong move in trying to make ourselves indispensable. Simply blending into human society... may be the best possible future for our race."

Natalie and I stayed silent, as the issue was too complex. We were Arites. We did not know how our race came to be or where our unusual abilities came from. We were immortal and practically invulnerable, but not capable of reproduction. There were very few of us, and that was our main secret. The great interstellar races would not reckon with us if they found out that there were no more than three hundred Arites remaining. And though just two centuries ago, there were more than seven hundred, the two-hundred-year war with the Iseyek seriously reduced our numbers. The insects took us with numbers, easily sacrificing hundreds of millions of soldiers just to destroy one Arite. Unlike our race, though, they were able to replace their losses. That is why we were very thankful to Crown Prince Georg. The peace treaty he helped us reach with the Swarm saved our race from extinction.

Three hundred Arites was all we had left. Saving those who remained was our main mission now. We could easily learn to blend in forever among billions of humans. All we had to do was keep our abilities a secret. After just a few centuries, everyone would forget that such a strange race had ever existed. Perhaps it really was worth thinking over Joan's words. After all, I also really liked being a human.

TRANSLATED FROM RUSSIAN BY ANDREW SCHMITT

THE BEST QUEST

A TALE FROM THE NEW *ALTERGAME* SERIES

BY ANDREW NOVAK

D UST HAS ONE indisputable advantage — it's impossible to get dirty. That was the thought that came to Jack's mind as he was walking across the Blighted Wasteland. The same idea applied to what was left of civilization after the Gendemic and the subsequent series of disasters. This little stub of a world was already impossible to stain. It was unlikely that someone could come up with something, which could make the world even smaller and even worse. Well, maybe there was. They could still disconnect Alterra. But that would just be beyond evil.

Alterra is the online game launched by the alpha-citizens of New Atrium and the last little island of civilization known to Jack. The alphas were so kind, in fact, that they even allowed the ghetto inhabitants to play — the ones who huddled around the protective Barrier of New Atrium. So that omegas, like Jack, got the idea that the world just might be bigger and cleaner than the piss-poor reality. Actually, as far as Jack was concerned, his own world was a bit bigger than that of most omegas.

Jack was a Walker. He wandered the Wasteland and searched the debris for something useful, anything that could be sold or used. He found mostly dust. But then, there was a lot of it.

Wherever he looked — only dust. That, and the rubble of a red-brick house. It was a two-hour walk from here to the ghetto borders. Pretty close, and these ruins had been searched probably a thousand times. They called this place Simon's House. Why? Jack didn't know. When he was still just starting to get out into the Wasteland, the ruins already went by this name.

Jack made for Simon's House and with every step, little clouds the ever-present dust puffed up from under his boots. Nothing here but dust... Though, what was that? Between the piles of bricks, sprinkled thickly with the same dust as everything else, something white peeked out. Jack involuntarily clenched the stick that he always kept with him while wandering the Wasteland – on the doorstep of Simon's House, white human bones were stacked in a neat pyramid. A skull topped the pile. In many Alterran dungeons, these types of little bone pyramids come back to life and turn into walking skeletons, guardians of the caves. Ugh! But this wasn't the game; it was reality... Here, bones don't come alive. They just placidly lay where the wild dogs had dragged them. This was just one of the Walkers, who decided to play a prank.

Well, the prank worked because everyone was familiar with Alterra. For some it was just for fun, but for many, Alterra was their only source of income. In-game gold could easily be converted into real money. Jack belonged to the minority and earned his money in real life. Alterra should remain a wonderland. He shook his head and walked past Simon's House. Today's haul was smallish, but it would be enough for a few days so he would not have to worry about food and could play at his leisure. Even a beer in the Rusty Rose would do. This seemed like a reasonable idea to Jack, so he adjusted the straps of his backpack and strode off to New Atrium. Go home, wash off the dirt, and then off to Alterra to drink a beer. That was the life.

It was a two-hour walk along the grey plains, then another hour and a half through the ghetto, where there was considerably less dust due to the wet winds from the sea. From here, the high wall of the Barrier was easily visible, New Atrium hidden behind it. They said that, once, the island had been called Manhattan... Once, very long ago, before the Gendemic, before the old world fell into the belly of hell. It was unclear what life is like in New Atrium. But most importantly, somewhere there, the **alphas**, residents of New Atrium, maintained Alterra. They kept the game on the servers, eliminated bugs, and once a year announced the Battle — the big quest, the prize for which was alpha-citizenship. And what **omega**, inhabiting the slums surrounding the Barrier, didn't dream about this? To leave behind the dirty trailers, the piles of rusty junk, the ruins of the old city — and enjoy all the amenities of civilization. A real beer, for example, and not the swill that they made in some places in the ghetto. The kind of beer that tasted like the beer they poured in Alterra.

Virtual beer tasted good and gave a small buff, but a temporary improvement in performance or taste weren't important. Jack went to the Rusty Rose to relax, distract himself, and overhear the news. At the next table, a group of players was loudly discussing their finished quests, recent in-game events, and occasionally, the goings-on in the real world. Jack went to the bar, where a burly barkeeper-NPC was pouring beer, took a mug, and settled into his favorite spot under the shadow of the wall. Where his back was covered and he could see who entered. Svetlograd – that's what they called the city – was a PvE zone, but habits are hard to break. Jack preferred these kinds of spots in reality, too.

He had arrived at the tavern a bit early — the crowd usually started to gather in late afternoon. At the moment, there were no more than ten people in the tavern and the musicians had only just started playing. Nighttime here would be lively, with songs and the drunken hubbub, but for now, everything was quiet. Just the thing after a difficult day. He sipped his beer, listening the outcome of the latest skirmish between the Kingdom of Maxitor and the necromancers of Nightmare, and simply enjoyed the peace and quiet.

A new group entered the tavern hall — three players, a Cleric and two Merchants. They were all regulars of the Rusty Rose and Jack knew them by sight, had even crossed paths with one of them in real life. The trio looked around the empty hall. The Cleric noticed Jack, smiled, and headed toward his table.

"Jack the Drifter! I thought you'd be here!"

"Hey, Mike."

One of the three went to the bar for beer while the others, without waiting for an invitation, sat themselves at Jack's table. Mike got right down to business.

"Jack, I have an offer for you. Wanna earn ten coins? A monthly quest opened up today — it's basically doing nothing for an hour. So?"

Jack swished the beer in his mug a bit, admired the elaborate patterns made by the liquid, and took a swig.

"What kind of quest? And why are you asking me?"

"We need someone with high-level strength. You're a Warrior. You fit the bill. I wanted to invite Jenkins... Do you remember Jenkins? But he's not in Svetlograd right now. Went off to Maxitor to fight necromancers and still hasn't come back. And we need someone stronger."

"But if you've all completed this quest already, then how will they give it to you again?"

Mike's second companion appeared and placed beer mugs in front of them.

"I haven't accepted the quest yet," explained Mike, grabbing his beer. "The other two in the group have taken it, but not me. So I'll take it this time. True, the game doesn't give the same quest to the same player. But those who have already finished the quest can stay in the group, and can repeat the task again that way, get it?"

They got distracted for a minute. Jack figured, why not? Not that he needed the coins. He'd just given the loot from the Wasteland to a buyer and taken his payment in game currency, so his wallet had more than two hundred gold. But if it was only for an hour, why not check out a new quest, eh?

"Alright," he nodded. "Tell me about it."

"Nothing to tell," Mike answered quickly. "There's a NPC merchant complaining that he bought his wife a bracelet and as soon as she put it on, she went ballistic — started attacking everybody, eyes crazy. Pretty much a typical case of possession. There was a spirit or demon of some kind locked in the bracelet... Here we showed up, two of us were holding her, the third was holding the husband, who was torn, wringing his hands and shouting at us not to hurt his dove. A dove, who, by the way, pushed me up against the wall and took off ten hit points. This was the first time we accepted the possession quest and didn't know what was going on. We've already gone through it twice, you know?"

Mike took a swig of beer and continued.

"In short, we need to hold the husband, too, so that he doesn't get in the way. And, well, like I said, someone should have high-level strength. The Cleric will hose the broad with holy water consecrated in the temple of Shining Vecta, she'll pass out and the ghost will come out of her, talking a lot of crap, but it's no big deal. The husband will shell out some coins..."

"How many coins?" asked Jack.

"Fifty."

"And I only get ten?"

"So what? This is our quest. We found it, explored everything we hadn't already checked; it was me that fat NPC beat against the wall. We're calling you in after everything's done."

"Okay, okay," Jack didn't want to argue. What a shame that the quest wasn't very exciting. "And what about the bracelet? What happens to it?"

"We also get that because the husband yells, 'I won't let my darling touch that dreadful little bauble. Get it out of my sight.' It really is just a cheap trinket. I'll take it to a merchant later and get three coins for it. So, are we going?"

Jack finished his beer and nodded. The three prospective quest participants exchanged their contact information with Jack to create the group and went outside. Svetlograd was amazing, as always. On the streets, there were richly dressed players and NPCs walking around, a priestess of Vecta in white here and there, sailors who brought rare items from the islands, merchants from Mal-Zaire dressed in exotic clothes and brightly colored feathered hats, and soldiers wearing heavy armor. Mages in voluminous robes were socializing, multicolored gems sparkled on sorcerers' fingers, and young beauties in low-cut dresses peeked out from coaches to check out the cavaliers' stats.

A few players were riding on mounts. Not really to use their pets, but to show off in front of the crowd. A knight in gilded armor on a huge white stallion watched jealously as a priest of the warlike Ged rode importantly by on his battle rhinoceros. Winged mounts were flying over the rooftops, their riders looking down at passers-by from above... Oh, yes, this place was something to be amazed by. And Jack delighted in the vibrant scene. He simply enjoyed the loveliness of the virtual world. In comparison with this splendor, what was the mud of the slums or the dust of the Blighted Wasteland? No, that wasn't real life. Alterra was.

Mike led the party through the center and went deeper into the poorer areas, where the artisans and small-time merchants lived. Here, of course, there was no particular splendor, but it was also something to see. All the houses were well kept with beautifully decorated facades and it was very rare that one saw two buildings that looked alike. The designers did first-rate work when they created Svetlograd.

"We're almost there already," Mike said over his shoulder to the rest of the group. "Only, when we start, you, Jack, stay on your toes. This chick will seem mellow, but then she'll tear out of their hands. Stay frosty."

Jack soon saw their future employer. A townsman was standing in the middle of the street and was speaking anyone who happened to pass by him too closely:

"Help me, good people! My wife's out of her mind! Taken over by some evil spirit! Someone help! Save her!"

Jack took a peek at his stats, out of pure

curiosity:

Jacob, Scand
Expertise: 25
Health: 30

Scands were a warrior people. They should be tall and broad-shouldered. Jack himself was playing a Scand and fit the racial characteristics quite well. But this NPC wasn't much to look at. Flabby, even. As a matter of fact, people of the game's Achaean race usually became merchants, but it seemed the developers decided to be original.

Mike walked up to the poor guy and blurted out,

"What's happened, good man?"

Then turned around and winked at Jack.

"Woe is me!" — Jacob wailed, now addressing a particular companion. "I bought a bracelet for my wife, thought I would treat my little dove. A beautiful one, with engraving. But as soon as she put the bracelet on, something emerged from it, like a kind of smoke or steam. And my darling became someone else, lunging at people, babbling nonsense. We were only barely able to force her upstairs and lock her in the bedroom. Now I don't know what to do. What can help her? She's possessed now."

"Don't worry, we'll fix it," snapped Mike, who had already heard this dialogue twice before. "We can help your wife by expelling the evil spirit that has taken hold of her body. You see, I'm a cleric, servant of the gods. I know about such matters. But this will not be an easy task."

"Help us, kind man! Save my wife!" Jacob begged. "Money is of no matter — I'll pay you fifty gold, if you'll only help her!"

Mike quietly reached an agreement with the NPC and just a minute later Jack received a quest group invitation.

> ***Join group***
>
> ***to complete the quest "Healing the Possessed"?***
>
> ***Yes / No***

He took the quest. Jacob brought the four saviors into his home and pointed out the ladder to the second floor. Measured, booming strikes resounded and the door at the top of the ladder shuddered.

While the distraught husband wailed, his eyes fixed on the door shaking under his wife's blows, Mike quickly assigned the roles. Jack and the stronger Merchant were supposed to hold the woman, while the second Merchant blocked interference attempts from the anxious Jacob, and Mike would cast out the spirit.

"Don't be shy," Mike issued one final instruction to Jack, "You can't hit this chick, but hold her with all you've got. All holds and sweeps are allowed. You'll see for yourself. This chick is as strong as a troll."

"Just be gentle with my beautiful girl," whined Jacob, "She is delicate!"

But no one paid attention to his pleas — they were preparing for the battle. All during the discussion, Mike was hammering home that this was a real fight; the quest only looked like a peaceful campaign. But the possessed woman actually was a dangerous enemy.

Finally, everybody was ready. The Merchants sucked down elixirs for buffs and Mike nodded at Jacob.

"Open the door, sir, and we'll take a look at your wife."

Jacob, glancing warily at the team of exorcists, climbed the ladder and pulled the latch. The door immediately swung open, nearly knocking him to the floor. A woman stomped determinedly down the ladder. She was much younger than her husband, round faced, and quite pretty. Jack barely had time to check her stats:

Milena, Scand.

Expertise: 15.
Health: 35.

He didn't get any further than that because, when he tried to intercept the woman, she tossed him aside with impressive force. However, Jack had been ready for such a turn of events. Mike hadn't repeated himself for nothing. Jack immediately blocked his opponent's path, grasped her around the waist with one hand and caught her wrist with the other. He'd wanted to disorient her with this hold, but it didn't work. If you grab a person like this, he will stop struggling whether he likes it or not because, otherwise, he'll twist his wrist and only cause himself pain. But this NPC was completely unfazed by it. Jack was swept out of her way. He had felt Milena's wrist breaking free of the hold.

A bracelet caught his eye. Probably the very one that had caused this mess. Indeed, just a trinket, a copper strip embossed in crude workmanship. The only thing that gave the little knickknack any value was the red gem. Inside the stone, a pale flame flickered rhythmically. Nothing happens by accident in Alterra. This flickering was probably supposed to mean that the stone was unusual, enchanted. Jack squeezed the woman's arm harder, but Milena still managed to push him out of the way and began to drag both Jack and the Merchant who gripped her other hand.

Jacob, watching this, was bouncing up and down, hands wringing.

"Oh, be careful, good people! Oh, you're holding her so roughly."

Milena twisted her left shoulder and shook the Merchant off, instantly making it more difficult for Jack to hold her. Jacob rushed in to help. Only it was unclear who to help. Either his wife or Jack. But it was much easier to hold him, since the townsman wasn't very strong and wasn't being impelled by a spirit dwelling inside him. The second Merchant held Jacob in place.

Jack felt the soles of his boots skidding across the floor. He rode behind the woman who powerfully and single-mindedly placed one foot after the other, never stopping. The interesting thing was, though, that when no one was standing in her way, Milena did not attack. She only tore away when someone tried to seize her hands. What for? Where was it taking her? There must be some purpose.

Mike the Cleric was fussing with a vial of holy water but couldn't find a good position.

Still grasping the wrist wearing the enchanted bracelet with all his might, Jack glanced at the wall the NPC was ploughing toward with the players clinging to her back. That had to be it! A luminous spot appeared on the wall, about hip high. It looked like a sunbeam, except the light from the windows didn't reach that far and there were no visibly shiny objects to reflect light. In fact, the pulsing of the light matched exactly with the rhythm of the twinkling stone in the bracelet.

At this point, Mike had finally managed to splash Milena with the water and shouted,

"In the name of blessed Vecta! Be gone, evil spirit!"

When the droplets fell onto Milena's face and chest, she froze on the spot, and Jack let out a sigh of relief. And then something happened to the NPC. She began to shake, her face turned white, while a thin haze appeared above her, like a bluish mist. The haze thickened in the air over the crown of her head, took on the silhouette of a human figure, and in a quiet, sepulchral voice said:

I, Beleth, have given an oath, vowing that I will neither deviate nor depart from this place so long as I have not obtained the Crown of Thergal for Annabelle the Beautiful... The oath lies in this bracelet, given to me by Annabelle. My oath is sacred and eternal.

"Alright, alright, you've made your point. Now take a hike," grinned Mike. "I mean, out with you. In the name of Vecta of the Light, leave here."

The misty figure grew faint and began to dissipate. Milena's eyes started to blink, looking around and noticing Jack and the others with surprise.

"Who are these people, Jacob? Why are you letting them touch me?" she babbled in a weak voice.

Your group has completed the quest "Healing the Possessed".
A reward of 50 gold can be received from the townsman Jacob.

Jack quickly released the NPC's arm and stepped back. The bracelet on the woman's wrist no longer gleamed and the flickering on the wall had disappeared, but Jack noticed that in the place where it had shone, a small stain remained. Not very noticeable, but still visible. Mike, grinning cheerfully, announced that the spirit had been exorcised, accepted the payment, took the bracelet from Jacob, who, as expected, wanted to be rid of it, and the entire party left the house.

When it was time to split the loot, Jack suggested,

"How about, instead of three coins of my share, I take the bracelet? As a keepsake. Never seen a possession quest before. Turns out, they're pretty fun."

Mike looked at him suspiciously, but Jack smiled widely with his most innocent expression, and the Cleric handed him the bracelet. Jack carelessly shoved the trinket into an inventory slot and suggested that they celebrate at the Rusty Rose. Although his companions thought that the exorcised ghost's words meant nothing, Jack had formed his own opinion on the matter. Annabelle the Beautiful was the founder of Svetlograd. There was a monument in her honor in one of the city squares. This was a notable character in the history of Alterra. Which meant that the quest associated with the ghost of Beleth should be a high-level quest.

And another thing — the possessed woman didn't attack people at all. She could hit and push only those who stood between her and the flickering spot on the wall, which was where she was actually trying to go. When Jack held her from behind, Milena didn't even try to turn around and attack. There wasn't any aggression in her behavior, just the drive to get to the mark on the wall. For what? The spot was somehow connected with the stone on the bracelet, since they both flared at the same time.

THAT EVENING in the Rusty Rose only began with the celebration of the successfully completed quest. At first, Jack sat at a table with the members of their temporary group. Then the party itself disbanded as each person found business at a neighboring table or the need to have a couple of words with someone from another group, and within an hour Jack was left alone. He quietly nursed a beer and occasionally glanced at the entrance. The person he needed usually appeared later.

The sky outside the window had darkened, the musicians on the podium were banging out the twentieth tune to count... and, finally, Stang made his appearance in the Rusty Rose

Stang, Areut
Level: 36
Health: 30

This guy was not a friend of Jack's. But they knew each other and had talked a few times. They both came the Rusty Rose fairly often and this was the only thing that linked them. Stang was a Thief and probably didn't keep many friends.

Jack waited until the Thief had settled at a free table, took two mugs from the barkeeper and joined him. Stang stared in surprise at the beer placed in front of him and slightly stiffened. People of his profession, as a rule, were not showered with gifts.

Jack winked.

"Don't worry, I'm not your fairy godmother and I'm not going to treat you to beer on a regular basis. I just need advice."

Stang relaxed.

"Go ahead, ask. Just don't expect me to give up professional secrets for a beer."

"Hmm, and I was counting on that... Okay, I'll get to the point. How does someone break into a townsman's house? Here, in Svetlograd?"

"Well, that depends on the citizen. There are houses, where secret infiltration is part of the quest. In those cases, you may encounter specific difficulties. There are vendors, who have warehouses and homes that are protected by magic spells. There are nobles' mansions that even I won't touch without good reason. Sometimes they're guarded by ghosts, sentry golems, or some other kind of particularly evil deviousness."

"And if it's only an unremarkable, small-time merchant or a master artisan's workshop? And there's nothing much to anticipate inside the home?"

"People usually don't rob those kinds of houses, unless they're really hard up," Stang squared his shoulders proudly. "Only a total noob would go that small. And I value my reputation enough to not waste my time on such nonsense."

"I wasn't talking about you. If I want to try something for the first time, then it would make sense to choose something simple."

"Going to switch professions?" Stang eyed his companion with a skeptical look. "You can't cut it. I can tell right away if a person has what it takes to be a thief or not. You're a Warrior, so stick with that."

"If I don't like it, I'll quit after the first try. But I should try at least once," said Jack.

"If the City Guard catches you, then they'll slap you with a fine or stick you in the slammer."

This was true. Svetlograd's City Guard were NPCs with ungodly defense bonuses and their health was 200 or higher. It was almost impossible to deal with them.

"Well, teach me, then, so that I don't get caught," Jack took a swig of beer. "I'll just sneak into the house, see what it's like. Probably won't even take anything."

"Strange desire. Well, if you only want to sneak into someone's house... Even a newbie like you could do it. You'll need this."

And Stang laid a weirdly bent steel rod on the table. Above the item, a message window appeared:

Universal Lockpick
Level: Common
Unlocks most residential buildings in Svetlograd with expertise up to 40.

"Twenty gold," added Stang.

"For a common item? No way."

"Try to get one yourself and you'll see — they don't come any cheaper," the Thief explained. "The price is so high because it's universal. You won't have to figure out the exact construction of the lock, plus it'll work for someone who hasn't leveled Lockpicking. If you don't want it, don't take it, but you asked a Thief for help, didn't you? So, here it is.

Transferring the coins, Jack carefully watched his companion's hands. You never knew what a thief was planning. Stang noticed his discomfort and laughed:

"Relax, I have a rule: never nick anything in the Rusty Rose". I come here to unwind, understand?"

"Well, if my field baptism is successful, I'll owe you a beer. And if your lockpick doesn't work..." he winked at the Thief, "then you'd better not catch my eye outside the city."

The lockpick migrated into his inventory and a message floated before his eyes:

You made a payment in the amount of 20 gold.

Would you like to see the transaction details?

Yes / No

You have 323 gold in your account.

Would you like to perform another transaction?

Yes / No

He clinked his mug with Stang's, marking the successful transaction. Jack sat for a while longer listening to the Thief's stories about his successful campaigns, then left the tavern.

At night, Svetlograd transformed. Everywhere, colorful lanterns burned, music played in taverns, and the number of people on the streets was no less than during the day. In the twilight, they looked even more picturesque and the luminous magical arts enchanting wizards' rings and circlets added a mysterious beauty to the picture.

Jack walked up and down the streets a few times to be sure that Stang hadn't followed him. You never knew what to expect from him... But it seemed that the Thief had remained at the Rusty Rose and wasn't going to follow. Which meant that it was time to get down to business.

It was already well after midnight and those still out on the streets were, for the most part, players. The NPCs had gone to bed for the night. The rare exceptions were those NPCs that the script had instructed to be nocturnal. In particular, the City Guard. Jack wandered for half an hour around the block where Jacob and Milena's house sat, waiting for the patrol with torches to pass by. Now he had at least half an hour at his disposal before the Guard would come back around to this street.

As for the owners of the house... Well, they were asleep. And unlike omegas, who were accustomed to sleeping very lightly, NPCs were guaranteed not to wake until morning. Well, if he didn't make too much noise. Jack wasn't planning on it. Jacob said that they had locked his wife in the bedroom, which was on the second floor. Which most likely meant that no one would be on the first floor.

Jack cautiously approached the door and pulled the lockpick out. When he slipped it into the keyhole, a new window with an image appeared at the top right of his vision: rollers and levers, and the shiny silver pin inserted between them. This was the inside of the lock and his lockpick. After a few turns, the prongs of the lockpick aligned with the lock pattern and a quiet click announced the successful Lockpicking attempt.

You have opened the lock. Used 1 attempt.
You have 9/10 uses of Universal Lockpick at your disposal.

Uh, Stang didn't mention that it was a limited resource. Though, on the other hand, it was fine. It worked on the first try and Jack wasn't planning on becoming a career Thief. He cautiously pushed the door and slipped into the darkness beyond it. Night in Alterra was drawn so that everything could be seen, while still keeping a sense of darkness. Jack stood for a minute, listening. Silence. The inhabitants were in the bedroom on the second floor. There was nobody on the first floor with Jack. He crept stealthily along the wall to the place, where he had noticed the spot that had glowed in time with flickering of the bracelet's stone. Well, and how was he supposed to find it in the dark? Jack pulled the bracelet out — nothing changed. The red stone didn't light up and nothing happened on the wall.

"Well, Beleth, how were you planning to do this?" Jack whispered.

At the mention of his name, the stone's

ghost reacted with a weak flicker.

"Beleth," Jack repeated, watching the wall intently, "Beleth, Beleth..."

Got it! On the wall, there was a barely noticeable stain, slightly lighter than the brickwork next to it. Jack touched the bracelet to the spot and the wall shook. Not the whole wall, of course, but something in it shifted and the overall image changed. Jack made out a crack in the wall and, extending his arm, pushed the bricks. He tried in one place, then another... There it was – part of the wall silently turned inward on invisible hinges, opening a passage into darkness.

Jack made out through the darkness the silhouette of steps and began to descend. The wall behind him shuddered again and clicked back into place. The crack behind him also disappeared.

"Guess it's only forward from here!" Jack proclaimed, continuing down the stairs.

A wave passed over the image before his eyes. What was that? Oh, an unexpected message appeared in chat. Jack wasn't expecting any news or anything. He stopped and opened the message. The window was dark grey, unusually designed, with some system icons at the bottom.

Greetings! The first stage of my quest has been solved. Congratulations. I say "my" because I was the one who developed it. And this is my best quest. By the way, welcome. To create Jacob's house, I digitalized my own home. So, in a sense, you are my guest. Feel free to make yourself at home. And when you've fully completed the quest, be sure to fulfill the task that needs to be done afterwards. Simon.Wenzowich@al-c.com

Jack, puzzled, paused on the stairs and re-read the message twice. Holy crap! For the first time in his career in Alterra, he'd received a non-default message from the current game administration — and it was a message from the developers themselves! What did that mean? Shaking his head, he continued down. This "Simon Wenzowich" had certainly died long ago. He'd lived and worked before the Gendemic, and even if he'd survived the catastrophe... How many years had passed since then? And that e-mail address format hadn't been used for a long time. Those services died out along with civilization. Too bad, of course. It would have been interesting to shoot the breeze with a real game designer. What was he thinking when he imagined Alterra? What had he wanted to say, when he drew the virtual world this way? There would be time later to think about it — after Jack reached the end of Beleth's quest.

The steps finally ended and ahead was total darkness, in which divergent tunnels could just barely be seen. He stood on a small platform, from which three pathways led into the gloom.

"Beleth!" Jack tried.

It didn't help. No sign came from the darkness. He chose the middle path and began to walk along it. And soon came to a trembling light. A torch was burning on the wall. It was hard to imagine that it had been lit recently. Especially considering the fact that the flame was violet. A magical fire lighting the way, that's what it was. Jack strode with more confidence and soon found himself on a platform from which another three tunnels branched off in different directions. The path in the middle was a bit brighter. There was another magical flame burning and both sides of the tunnel were lined with white bones. Piles of them, each topped with a skull. But this wasn't the Blighted Wasteland. It was quite clear what was about to happen here. As soon as Jack moved toward the middle tunnel, the bones creaked nastily into motion. Two skeletons stood up on each side of the pathway. Above each one appeared:

Dungeon Guardian
Expertise: 10
Disease: 20

As Jack stepped toward them, the skeletons stepped in his way. One threw a hand forward, its sharp bones ripping through the air, but Jack was ready. He ducked, stepped back, and kicked his opponent back into the other skeleton. Their bones jumbled, intertwined. Jack ran over and destroyed the resulting ridiculous two-headed figure with a few punches, smashing it against the wall.

Afterwards, he continued down the tunnel. Ahead there was a grinding rattle, as if two rough pieces of iron were rubbing against each other. Jack had already seen the burning torch with violet fire when a skeleton appeared, coming at him. This one was more impressive, with rusty steel bands on its wrists. Pieces of chain hung from the bands and the skeleton's right claw was clamped around a curved knife, also rusted and very sinister looking.

Dungeon Guardian
Expertise: 20
Disease: 30

Jack withdrew his sword from his inventory. He used a "bastard" sword, which was long enough to swing with both hands if necessary. Against the dead warrior, it was just an excessively long blade to keep the enemy at a distance while Jack smashed its skull and shattered the skeleton to pieces. He turned around when he heard a rattle from behind.

A second skeleton, armed with a heavy axe, had crept up behind him. Jack managed to get his sword under the blow and drove his enemy back. With a few thrusts, he forced it to break its guard and plunged the tip between the skeleton's ribs, then teased and slammed the impaled bones into the wall. The dead soldier scattered with a clatter, but once again from the hallway came the scrape and rattle of more bones. Enemies were approaching from both directions. Jack stepped back to the torch. There, at least, it was brighter. He could see the corridor from here. At equal intervals, roughly every seven or eight steps, alcoves extended along both sides, each one holding a skeleton. They were moving, ripping out the rusted chains that were fastened to steel rings embedded in the walls. Bending down, one picked up a knife, another an axe, and they shuffled forward.

And in the distance, the purple light of the next torch fluttered. Could he fight his way through to it? Jack moved down the corridor towards the sluggish Guardians. He had to spend about a minute on each one, but luckily the hallway was so narrow that he could fight one mob at a time. Jack dispatched five opponents, reached the next torch, and saw that the next alcove was a pass-through that ended at a set steps leading down.

He fled downstairs. The Guardians, their bones awkwardly dropping on the narrow steps and rusted weapons scraping the walls, followed after him.

"Must be fun for you guys, Jacob and Milena, living with these folks... Yeah, and Simon Wenzowich definitely had an interesting cellar."

Jack ran to the torch burning just ahead, hurrying to stay ahead of the slow-moving undead. He ran so fast that the next opponent to come forward barely had time to raise its shield. This skeleton was in plate armor, rusted and bent. Jack slammed his shoulder into the shield and the sent the skeleton blocking his path spinning.

Dungeon Guardian
Expertise: 30
Disease: 50

The hit was diseased.

You receive damage!
You lose 4 hit points!

Jack hadn't even noticed that the rusty blade had stuck him, but a rivulet of red flowed down his side.

You lose 2 hit points!

And the skeleton was already approaching with its sword raised. Jack quickly attacked, forcing his enemy to step back. Crouching low, he rushed forward and the skeleton's weapon swung over his head. Lunging, he struck its bony legs. The dead soldier staggered and he dealt another strike from above on its helmet, putting all of his strength into it.

You lose 1 hit point!

The wound continued to bleed, leeching his hit points. And behind him was the approaching clatter of dry bones and the scrape of rusty iron.

Jack raised his sword again. The skeleton in front of him stepped back and shielded its head. Then he lunged powerfully at it and smashed his shoulder into the shield while his sword, held with both hands, slipped in under the shield. His weapon parried the skeleton's rusty blade and passed through bones, crushing them. *Shake off the clinging bones to the blade and move forward.* Jack drank a healing elixir on the go, filling his health bar.

Near the next torch, another Guardian in rusted chainmail was waiting. Jack was prepared for this one. He was well ahead of his pursuers and could dispatch the skeleton at his own pace, according to the rules of swordplay.

Well, where was the exit? The recess near this torch was ordinary — no steps leading down. He'd have to run to the next one. Jack swore out loud. There were two skeletons here, each with expertise in the thirties. But there was no alcove with a passage behind them, just a thick plank door fastened with steel strips. The door looked solid enough to block his pursuers... if, that is, he could take care of the pair of Guardians in front of him.

He had to take care of them, and quickly, for the passage here was wider and, if the undead shambling in the narrow corridor behind him reached this place... Jack rushed his opponents, swinging his sword hastily. One skeleton shielded himself behind a buckler and Jack, putting all of his strength and inertia behind it, struck with his sword. The enemy flew back, its bones rattling inside the rusty cuirass. The second tried to pierce Jack from the side and nearly got him.

You receive damage!
You lose 3 hit points!

The fallen skeleton stirred, the scattered bones were reassembling themselves into a human form. Jack dodged another attack from the still-standing skeleton and jumped onto the one lying on the ground. His boots skidded with a squeak along the rusty cuirass, something cracked beneath them, and bones once again scattered to the sides. Jack, stamping the prostrate ghoul and kicking aside its bones, turned to face off with the remaining skeleton. It didn't back down, but pushed forward, as if it were trying to drive Jack away from its fallen comrade.

And the wounds left by the rusty blades continued to bleed.

You lose 2 hit points!

Another Guardian emerged from the darkness and stepped into the area lit by the violet flame of the torch. Jack had finally managed to stab the persistent undead. He immediately darted over to this new enemy and with a wide stroke, decapitated the skull with the helmet still attached, then turned toward the door. The skeleton lying on the ground just wouldn't settle down and was again beginning to reassemble its pieces. Its skull clanged inside the mangled helmet visor. The skeleton began to rise. Jack hastily kicked it, slammed it on the rocks, and planted the sharp blade into the visor slot.

The bones froze for a heartbeat, then fell and scattered. Jack hopped over to the door and pushed. Nothing happened. It was locked. He'd have to kneel and switch out his sword for the Universal Lockpick. Once again a window appeared with the image of the lock interior and he wiggled the silver squiggle inside. Something cracked in Jack's hands, but the door remained closed.

Failed. Used 1 attempt.
You have 8/10 uses of Universal Lockpick at your disposal.

Well, of course. This lock was more complicated than the latch of a law-abiding citizen under level 40.

Failed. Used 1 attempt.
You have 7/10 uses of Universal Lockpick at your disposal.

The bony knocking and rattle sounded very close now, but Jack didn't let himself get distracted. He impatiently turned the lockpick in the keyhole. He'd already kind of figured out how to insert it, so that as many rollers as possible were compressed in the picture in the corner of his field of vision. Now the sound of bones crunching was right in his ear!

Jack waited half a second and then leaned his whole body to the side. Over his shoulder, a rusty sword was sticking out of the door and he sharply thrust his elbow backwards. He struck something hard and, judging by the rolling clatter behind, sent the Undead Guardian flying.

Another turn of the lockpick and -

You have opened the lock. Used 1 attempt.
You have 6/10 uses of Universal Lockpick at your disposal.

Overhead something started to rasp again. Jack saw movement above him out of the corner of his eye, leaned on the door... and flew into the darkness with the skeleton, which couldn't stay on its feet due to the inertia of its own strike.

They both fell onto the floor slab, Jack and the Undead Guardian, but the player was faster. He rolled over, struck its visor with his elbow, and bought himself a few seconds to withdraw his sword. Lying on the ground, he slashed at the pile of bones and rusty iron, which were languidly gathering back into fighting condition. The skull, knocking around inside the twisted helmet, rolled off to the side and he jumped up.

He stepped to the door to shut it. In the

opening, the yellow-toothed, grinning mug of another Guardian poked in. Jack drove it back with a strong kick, closed the door, fumbled with the bolt and slid it into the slots. A blow fell on the door from the other side, but the skeleton didn't have the power to break the iron-banded boards of this door. The game wouldn't allow it.

Having shaken off his pursuers, Jack took a look around. He was in a chamber. Finally, no more narrow corridors but some kind of open room. Rows of columns ran deep into the area, lit by violet torch flames. If there were no walls, then there were no alcoves in the walls, which meant there were no chained Guardians, who freed themselves easily from their chains. Having sorted out where he was, Jack checked his health bar. Frankly speaking, the sight didn't please him — little more than half. He'd started with 45 hit points, armor bonuses all together gave him another 10%, but now he was left somewhere in the neighborhood of thirty. Those skeletons banged me up pretty good. What now? Sit and wait while he regenerated? No, because night wouldn't last forever and in the morning, Jacob and Milena would come down to the first floor. What if he had to leave the dungeon through their house? Which was actually the digitized house of Simon Wenzowich.

There were still health elixirs, but only two,

and they only gave five points of health each. It wasn't enough. Jack sighed heavily and very slowly wandered between the rows of columns. He couldn't take any more risks — his health was too low for another battle. And there would be at least one more battle. It wasn't possible that this quest would end without a boss encounter. Jack, without needlessly hurrying, walked from torch to torch. Rows of columns materialized from out of the darkness, the chamber continued on. He held his sword ready, but nothing came at him. It even got a bit boring... but then an arch appeared in the darkness ahead. Finally, something.

The arch turned out to be an exit. Well, what else could it be? The chamber couldn't be endless. Nearby, a chest sat under a wall. Jack looked around and opened the lid. There were three items in front of him: a bottle with a dark blue liquid, a magnificent snow-white feather, and a faded bouquet tied with a red ribbon. Pinned to the underside of the lid was a scrap of parchment. The inscription on it read:

Choose one item and enter.

Jack began to inspect the proffered gifts. If he held his gaze on an item, an information window would appear. It was clear what the dark blue bottle was:

Elixir of Health, single use, +10

Not bad, of course. It was just what he needed after dealing with the Undead Guardians. The feather also looked tempting.

Helmet Plume, +10% power Duration: 1 hour. Cooldown: 2 hours

Clearly not out of place, if there's going to be a boss encounter. But the bouquet was less obvious.

Bouquet — the best gift for a lady. It will make her feel dreamy.

"Simon, what are you up to?" Jack muttered. "The first two items are clearly useful in my situation. The third one is just absurd. Just as absurd as a basement full of evil skeletons under the home of the peaceful, Mr. Nice Guy Jacob and his gentle dove, Milena. The way I see it, decision is clear: I've got to take the useless flowers. But isn't the hint too obvious? No, it's not. You already know that I'm gonna run and fight. So now I have only one thing in mind: run farther and fight even more. But if you've screwed me over, Simon Wenzowich, I'll... I'll just call you a lot of bad names because you're already dead."

Jack took the bouquet. The chest lid slammed shut and the door in the arched passageway very slowly vanished with a bone-chilling screech, inviting him to enter.

With the bouquet in hand, he stepped into the opened passage. To say that he felt like an idiot would be an understatement. In the upper right above his head, his health bar loomed, just under two thirds full. His bastard sword seemed too puny for whatever he would find behind that door.

He was right. The next room was downright tiny and a pair of Guardians were waiting for him a couple of feet from the threshold. Jack instantly realized that he wouldn't have been able to handle this, not even at full health or with increased strength.

Across from the door stood a skeleton with long icy-blond curls and it wore a heavy dress of gold brocade. A silver girdle decorated with dark blue and green stones was tied around its extremely thin waist. Its bodice was also decorated with gems. The dress would be suited, perhaps, for a queen.

In her bony, ring-studded fingers the dead woman held a heavy morning star. Its heavy club end was covered with curved blades, similar in shape to grappling hooks. The weapon burned with that violet light, obviously of magical and incredibly dangerous origin.

Dead Necromancer Leonora
Expertise: 45
Disease: 50

Behind her, looming like statues, were two soldiers clad head to toe in black armor. Heavy steel gauntlets rested on the hilts of two-handed swords. The slits in the helmet visors winked with the violet fire. The guardians' stats read:

Dead Knight of Thergal
Expertise: 40
Disease: 80

Without any doubt, there was no chance against this trio. The woman lifted her head with a bony creak and readily picked up the mace. With this movement, the glow that emanated from the weapon swirled up in rings. The knights clenched their swords and moved closer to the matriarch.

Jack actually shivered when the holes in the skull beneath the fair curls stared at him. Really creepy when something like that looks at you. Yeah, and those light gold curls on bare bones were a wild combination. Well, Simon, you had quite the imagination. Maybe you just hated blondes?

He carefully moved toward the bony Leonora, extending the wilted bouquet. The skeleton raised its club and Jack winced — it didn't work! But then the skeleton shook its head and there was a brief flash of fire in its eye sockets. As if something had responded in the wight's bony soul... Dropping the club, the skeleton raised its other hand in a jerky, mechanical movement, took the flowers, and brought them to its nonexistent nose. The Necromancer Leonora shivered, her shoulders slumped, and the mace fell, its hooks scraping the floor. The knights behind her simultaneously stepped aside, opening the way. Jack, without removing his hands from his sword handle, passed between the undead and went to the next door. His heart pounded as he passed the sinister trio...

Next was the throne room, if you could call it that. Richly decorated, carved walls surrounded a podium with a tall chair, which was also carved with skulls, snakes, spiders and other similarly fun things. In front of the throne were two skeletons, which were interlocked in a strange embrace. One, wearing a crown and gold-embroidered attire, had closed its bony fingers around the throat of the other, which was dressed like a soldier. The warrior's sword pierced its crowned enemy, the blade slicing between the ribs.

Beleth the Knight
Supreme Necromancer Thergal

No expertise or any other indicators. These dead men were not coming back to life.

"End of the road?" Jack asked. "Where's the thundering fanfare? And there's no one coming to greet me, to tell me that the quest is completed? So, is there something missing?"

He took a few steps and stopped over the figures. The crown fell from Thergal's head and rolled to Jack's feet.

Crown of Thergal
Level: Legendary

The crown was gold and heavy-looking. It was rimmed with sharp teeth, slightly curved inwards over the top. Along the rim was a checkered pattern of alternating red, blue and green gems. The crown was emitting a soft glow.

Nothing else was available to loot. Their clothes and gear were a part of the drawn images.

"But still no 'quest completed' message."

Jack noted when the crown had been placed in his inventory. "So what else is there? Oh, yeah!"

He pulled out Beleth's Bracelet, the remaining piece from the possession quest, and fastened it on the dead knight's wrist.

Attention!
You have completed the hidden quest "The Crown of Thergal"
You receive +1 XP.
You have 28 XP
Earn 2 XP to unlock new skills.

Skills — in other words, specific racial abilities that are given for every ten experience points a player gets, and Jack had just made a decent step toward this award.

A rat jumped out of the darkness, tore the bracelet off the skeleton's hand, and briskly ran off toward the throne. Jack took off behind it and managed to see the rodent disappear into a low, narrow tunnel. There was a staircase leading up. And here was the exit. Nice. Now he wouldn't have to go back through the skeleton-filled dungeon and the house with peacefully sleeping NPCs.

Climbing the stairs after the rat, Jack realized that it had shown him how Beleth's Bracelet kept making its way back to the world of the living. The circle had closed. The bauble, carried to the surface by the rat, would somehow be picked up by a jewelry merchant, Jacob would buy the little thing for his dove, and the restless spirit of the knight Beleth would possess her. After all, Beleth swore his unbreakable oath on this very bracelet and spoke about it before being struck down by the exorcism. In Alterra, everything was planned. It was all linked to a single story.

Jack emerged through a narrow access hole onto the street and looked around. It was strange to see the sleeping city before dawn. Below, Dead Soldiers with rusty blades wandered, the bony Leonora who was dreaming of something over a wilted bouquet... and everyone up here was asleep. Well, maybe not everyone. Almost everyone. The Guards, armor clanging, were striding evenly by torchlight through a sleeping Svetlograd. The thief Stang was sneaking through some stranger's home, shoveling loot into his inventory slots... all while the others were sleeping peacefully. The NPCs Jacob and Milena, for example. Here, by the way, was their house — about twenty feet from Jack. It was odd that at the end of all his wandering belowground, Jack returned almost to its starting point. That same red-brick house...

Wait, hold on. Red-brick house? The

digitized home of Simon Wenzowich? Simon's House in the Blighted Wastelands, two hours from the outskirts of the ghetto in reality? It couldn't be... But couldn't it?

Jack would have broken out in a sweat, if this feature had existed in the game. Well, it could be! Simon's House. It wasn't often that wasteland ruins had a proper name, but Simon's House has been called that for ages. Probably ever since the first Walkers still remembered the names of the leading developers of Alterra.

"Now this is something to think about," Jack said to himself. "Maybe in Mr. Wenzowich's house you won't wind up in the dungeon where the necromancer Thergal is hidden, but there is definitely a basement. Anyway, it could be. These ruins were well known to all Walkers, and everyone was certain that there was nothing there, that it had been explored long ago. At any rate, I was certain of it, and I'm not more stupid than anyone else. And if it never occurred to me to search the basement... Why hadn't it occurred to me? And how it came! It's just dawned on me. I just need to grab a flashlight and spare battery. What if the basement turns out to be half the size of the dungeon of Thergal's? Simon, did you invite me over? Thanks, I'll have a look around. You know what? Well done, Simon Wenzowich. You didn't exaggerate in your chat message: this really was the best quest."

A DAY LATER, Jack was standing in front of Simon's House, trying to find some similarity between these time-eaten ruins and Jacob's tidy little house. The wind was sweeping across the Wasteland and bands of dusts slithered like grey snakes around Jack's legs, lifting the flaps of his loose cloak.

"You never know until you try," Jack said to himself. "At any rate, no one's going to see me, so no one will laugh when I don't find anything."

He walked around the ruins and crossed over what remained of the threshold. This would be Jacob's living room. There was nothing left of the staircase, but if it had ever existed... then he'd have to look there in that wall. Jack crossed the room and sat against the wall.

"Beleth," he said quietly and put his hand on the bricks.

Magic in the real world doesn't exist. It just happened that one brick shifted easily at the first touch. It wasn't any kind of secret. You just needed to know where to look. Jack stuck his fingers in the newly formed hole and pulled. Dust spilled out and a rectangular section of the wall opened up like a door. A staircase lead down, the steps lost in the darkness. Here it was. The basement.

Jack turned on the flashlight and began go down. The basement, of course, turned out to be normal-sized and there was nothing magical. A square room, lined with old computers and shelves filled with all kinds of electronic junk.

Faded posters advertising a new game world hung on the walls. A beefy barbarian in a crested helmet poked his axe at the viewer: "Have the guts to take me on?" A brunette with a barely-covered, voluptuous bust held a flickering flame in the palm of her hand and winked: "Wanna see my magic?" A grey-bearded priest in a wide mantle scowled: "The secrets of Alterra await you!"

Web designer Simon Wenzowich had built himself a work space away from all the noise and had worked here in peace and quiet. Jack passed his flashlight over the room, scanning the game characters on the posters and trying to guess the uses of the various devices on the shelves.

In the far corner across from the stairs stood a massive table, a chair with armrests next to it. There was a dust-covered monitor on the table, an ancient VR headset, a tangle of wires, some long-since obsolete gadgets... Jack, moving the flashlight, passed between the racks and sat down in Simon's chair. Where was the computer tower? Under the table? Yep, there it was. And the power supply, the cables of which led to a dust-covered outlet in the wall. He bent down and flicked the switches. Nope. Of course, everything had been here for a long time and was certainly dead. But it would have been cool to see what was left on the computer desktop of a developer of Alterra.

Seeing a whitish corner sticking out from under the cables on the table, he pulled on it and extracted an antique photograph that had been colored once, but now had almost completely faded. In it... Damn!

In it was the merchant Jacob, his wife, and a little girl. I mean... there were three regular people standing somewhere in a park, against a background of trees. They were smiling. They were happy together. And two of the faces — Jacob's, in whom the long-dead developer had encapsulated his own appearance, and his wife's, although younger than in the game — Jack recognized at once.

Hold on, he thought, I have a spare battery. I wonder if there's enough of a charge. Gotta try.

After a quarter of an hour spent messing with cables and plugs, he anxiously reached again for the switch. Come on, help me out, gods of Alterra... Jack jabbed the button and froze, listening closely. For a few moments nothing happened, and he heard only the resounding thud of his heart. Then a thought flashed: well, he had been counting on a miracle. It had been stupid to hope. He could find a thousand reasons why it didn't work — the computer was fried, the battery didn't have enough of a charge, a bad cable connection... Could have been anything. But then the computer clicked on, the light on the front of the CPU block under the table lit up, the cooling fan roared wildly, and a dim spot appeared in the center of the monitor. It began to spread across the screen, system messages ran...

Jack sighed. Miracles still happened sometimes! They happened rarely, so that people didn't forget to appreciate them. And in front of him the strange, ancient interface was slowly coming to life. The desktop was pristine, except for the Recycle Bin icon in the corner and, right in the center, a lonely little file: "a letter to my daughter.txt". Jack rummaged through the serpentine tangle of cords and extracted the mouse. He opened the file and began to read.

Annabelle, daughter. Tomorrow you will be sixteen years old and will enter Alterra. If you only knew how I've waited for the day when you could finally appreciate what your dad does.

I'll never be able to forgive myself for not being with you on this day. But you already know that the new quarantine law is very strict. I have to stay at the clinic for evaluation. There are already orderlies here in hazmat suits and masks. They're waiting for me to finish this message and copy it to e-mail so that they can take me away. And I barely begged that off these stubborn people, can you believe it? I'm certain that I've not been infected, sitting here in the basement but, for some reason, they're anxious and are rushing me.

I'm so sorry that I won't be there tomorrow to wish you a happy birthday. You know that your mom left me long ago and took you with her... I had hoped for a long time that she would change her mind and come back, that this was the act of someone temporarily possessed, but... alas. Well, you'll be able to see your mama in the game, too. And me. All of us have found a place there. And here's the most important thing: I've made a present for you. When you're comfortable in Alterra and have had your fill of the beauty of Svetlograd, do this. Find the merchant, Jacob, on Trader's Row and accept the quest from him. I'm sure that, unlike other players, you'll understand its hidden meaning and go further, where others won't. You will seek out the Crown of Thergal and lay it on the brow of the statue depicting princess Annabelle. Whose appearance do you think I used for this statue?

Do you remember the nighttime story I used to tell you? About the fair princess Annabelle, the brave knight Beleth, and the evil sorcerer Thergal? After so many years, my stories have come to life in Alterra.

Well, that's it. That's everything. The orderlies are demanding that I hurry up. Happy birthday, darling, and do what I've written here. Put the crown on the statue's head. I guarantee you won't regret it! Something special is waiting for you. It's a shame that I can't give you the gift myself, but nobody has ever gotten such a birthday present. You'll see, it'll be amazing.

I can already hear the footsteps behind me, but I still need to copy the file. I love you.

Your...

The fan at last snorted and died. Under the table something clicked and the screen went blank. For a few minutes, Jack just remained in place, staring ahead thoughtfully. He thought about the old world. It probably had been so beautiful and fair, but forever lost, swept away by the genetic storm of global catastrophe... He wondered, were there any other entrenched islands of civilization like New Atrium? With dirty, moldy crusts of ghettos clinging to them, like the place where he lived? And did the local non-citizen omegas play in Alterra or its equivalent, which the alphas threw at them, like a shiny, lacquered, artificial bone, so that they wouldn't revolt?

Then he shuddered, came to his senses, and at last looked around. He touched the ancient computer display in parting, climbed the stairs, and carefully closed the hidden door behind him. Goodbye, my friend, Simon, creator of the best quest.

Once outside, Jack circled Simon's House to be sure that no one had seen his secret. The Blighted Wasteland — the place wasn't too crowded, and right now he couldn't see anyone nearby.

Then he strode off toward New Atrium and the ghetto. His thoughts were still far away. He pictured Simon Wenzowich, his "possessed" wife, and his daughter Annabelle, who was depicted in a statue in the center of Svetlograd. No, poor Simon could not, did not have time to tell his daughter how to find the Crown of Thergal, and she never placed the artifact on the head of her statue in virt. The sculpture was standing in the square without its crown. Maybe they cut off the electricity too soon or old Simon was forcibly dragged from the computer. Or perhaps the email was sent, but his beloved daughter hadn't read it... Then the Gendemic began, civilization collapsed, and all plans, hopes, and expectations went down the tubes. And Alterra remained. Only it was able to survive the catastrophe. And in a square in Svetlograd, a statue of Annabelle

Wenzowich still stands. Waiting for its crown. Waiting for the miracle that a father promised his daughter.

Jack was thinking about how ridiculous he would look, clambering up the statue to put the Crown on its head. He'd have to do it at night. So no one would see.

TRANSLATED FROM RUSSIAN BY KRYSTAL DIEHL

THE DATE

A TALE FROM
THE MIRROR WORLD SERIES

BY MARINA AND ALEXEY OSADCHUK

"HA! THERE HE IS, my competition!"

We both turned to the sound of Count's voice. A scraggy dwarf had just left Beast's office and was now looking around himself in surprise.

Today of all days the reception was packed with all sorts, NPCs as well as players. They spoke in loud voices, laughing and cracking jokes, sharing their experiences of the Caltean attack on the Citadel. For many of them, this had been their first event — which meant they had a lot to take in.

A scraggy dwarf... actually, was he a dwarf at all? I took a better look. How funny. Nickname: Olgerd. Race: Ennan. Not another dead race! Apparently, he didn't want to publicize the fact. His dwarven disguise must have cost him a pretty penny. How very interesting.

Despite being a newb, the guy definitely had an agenda. Then again, who hadn't? Grinders didn't come to the Citadel to admire the local scenery.

"Count, look at this Digger!" Turbo growled. "He's definitely not digging it, is he?"

I cast a sideways glance at him. Turbo was our tank. He may have looked fearsome but he was in fact a kind, helpful kind of guy. With friends, anyway.

With a startle, the fake dwarf looked in our direction. A serious, studying look. In all my time in the game, I'd already got used to these kinds of stares. I may be a cute twenty-year-old girl in real life but here I'm a power to be reckoned with. A full set of Purple gear. Level 200+. It's true what they say about Mirror World — or the Glasshouse, as we call it — that this particular virtual world opens up a wealth of opportunities, allowing you a taste of a totally new lifestyle.

"Whatcha stalling for, Dwarf?" Count flashed him a pearly smile. "Let's get to know each other."

"Pleased to meet you," the Ennan ventured a smile.

"The event sucked," Turbo growled. "Nothing to write home about. Still, you did a good job."

The Ennan gave him a wary look.

"Guys, leave the poor Grinder alone," I said as softly as I could.

He nodded his gratitude. His stare alighted briefly on my crossbow. I know, I know. I love it too.

If only he'd seen the beast we'd had to smoke in order to lay our hands on this delightful thingy! Had it not been for Count, we'd all have gone home with our tails between our legs.

I smiled to him. "Please don't take any

notice of them, Olgerd. It's just that we've wasted two days already on these ridiculous mini-events. We've come here to get us some scalps. Instead, we're hunting mobs."

Judging by the look on his face, he didn't consider the Caltean attack a mini-event. He had a point. The difference was, the first time I'd come to the Citadel I'd already been level 100. I still didn't like thinking about it. And this zero-level guy had managed to hit it big on his first day here, ending up on the event's top player list. I really needed to keep an eye on him.

Count seemed to be thinking in the same direction. I, of all people, recognized this glint of interest in his eye.

"I see," the Ennan said non-committedly.

"How's the Beast?" Turbo asked him.

"How's who?" he looked clueless.

We exchanged understanding glances. "We can see you're a newb," Count said.

"Beast is what we call Gard," I explained. "He may be an NPC but he's a sick bastard."

"Yeah," Turbo agreed. "He makes you wait for a quest like it's some lottery draw."

In the time that we stood there, several NPCs had walked past. Each of them thought of slapping Olgerd's shoulder or saying something along the lines of "Keep up the good work!"

Been there, heh. Got the T-shirt.

Seeing his embarrassed reaction to praise, Count added with a grin, "Don't be shy. It's always like this when you get a medal. Tomorrow it'll calm down. That's the admins' way of encouraging players to strive for new heights."

"Do you mean that tomorrow they won't be so friendly with me anymore?" Olgerd asked.

"Oh yes they will," Count replied. "They'll still have respect for you but it won't be as explicit. Medals are a great thing. You should do all you can to get new ones and upgrade the old ones."

"Thanks for the tip."

What an interesting individual. Very. I really should invite him to join us at the inn. We needed to talk. From what I'd heard, our clan needed some advanced mine diggers. And this Olgerd seemed to be taking his profession seriously. Also, his latest achievement spoke for itself.

I was about to blurt all this out when Gard's adjutant growled,

"Olgerd! The Captain will see you!"

"What a shame," I said when the door of Gard's office closed behind him.

"Meaning?" Turbo asked.

"Interesting guy, don't you think?" Count asked me, ignoring his question.

I nodded. "Quite. I've been toying with the

idea of asking him to join us at the inn."

"You sure?" Turbo butted in again. "What's so interesting about him?"

Count rolled his eyes. "Well, for one, he's one of the dead races."

"What, a dwarf?"

I shook my head in disbelief. Turbo! He'd never change. Then again, if you needed to have someone chopped in two with a poleaxe, Turbo was your man.

Now Count, despite his quite flashy name... he was, how can I say it... he was *different*.

His gear was awesome. He'd done the Captain level in Valor. He'd taken part in the Great Battles. Count was our clan's elite, pure and simple.

But still he was a good friend, ready to help you out at a moment's notice.

Most of our clan's girls were crazy about him.

You can't imagine how many of them had tried to set him up for a real-life date. No such luck. He even avoided our clan's powwows.

At first many guys had laughed at us saying we'd fallen for a cute avatar, implying he might be a right uglie IRL. Others said that Count had used his own appearance for his char. The only difference being, he probably had only two hands and a lighter shade of skin, LOL.

I didn't give a damn about his looks. As long as he was the same kind of guy as he was here in the game, what else did you need?

A touch to my shoulder awoke me. Oh. I'd been away with the fairies, apparently. It had been happening to me too often just lately.

"Irene? You all right?"

Count's right hand alighted on my shoulder. His emerald eyes betrayed concern.

I nodded. "I'm fine. Lagging a bit, that's all."

"It happened to you before, didn't it?" Turbo butted in. "You need to contact support. It could be your capsule playing up."

"I will," I said, hiding my eyes.

An awkward pause hung in the air. Or was it my imagination? Finally, Turbo coughed loudly. "I don't know about you but I'm not staying. It looks like Beast is stuck with this Grinder for a while. I might come back in the evening."

"Sure. Suit yourself. Hope you don't mind if we wait for a bit. You never know."

Did Count's voice really tremble?

Turbo shrugged. His observational skills weren't that great. He bade his goodbyes and headed out.

Count watched his burly back disappear. Then he turned to me, his voice suddenly strained. "Are you doing something tonight?"

"Dunno," I replied matter-of-factly. "Why,

you have any ideas? Know any new dungeons?"

I tried to stay calm but some of Count's anxiety must have rubbed off on me. What was going on?

He heaved a sigh. "No," he shook his head, "I don't. I wondered if you would like to go out tonight. In real life, I mean."

* * *

THE CAPSULE'S TOP slowly began to rise.

I opened my eyes.

The room was bathed in soft shadows, the way I liked it when I logged out. The walls and the ceiling were specked with red and blue reflections of the control panel lights.

I drew in air, taking in my home smells. The door was slightly ajar. My room may have been far from the kitchen but not far enough for me to miss the aroma of Mom's pies.

My mouth began to water. *Yum...*

I listened intently. Four sets of claws were clattering over the parquet floor, meaning that Mom's radio receiver had worked, sending Mickey my way.

The door swung open. Mickey the beagle was standing there, his brown ears splayed, his square head cocked to one side. He wasn't yet sure whether I was already awake. His moist black nose pulsated fast. If a dog could sniff you to death, it had to be a beagle.

I pretended I was still asleep, watching him from under my eyelashes. Mickey shifted his feet undecidedly, licking his chops. He must have already received some treat in the kitchen. Everything about him seemed to say, *Come on now, get up already! Let's go to the kitchen! There're so many tasty things there! They might disappear while you're lying here all alone!*

Finally, I raised my head and gave him a smile.

Oh, the celebration! His signature bark echoed through the house, informing everyone I was back. His black and white tail rotated like a fan, sending his entire body into a frenzy.

He approached the capsule and laid his front paws on its edge, his mouth gaping, his ears drooping down to his neck in a most funny way.

"That's my smiler!"

We spent the next few minutes hugging until the oven clicked shut in the kitchen. Mickey disappeared in a flash, afraid of losing out on a treat. He wouldn't miss it for the world.

"Reeny?" Mom called me. "You want some coffee, sweet?"

Excellent. Only a few days ago, she'd have already been upon me, desperate to help her handicapped daughter to vacate "this crazy contraption".

"Yes, please!" I called back. "I'm coming!"

Let's do it, then. I grabbed at the railings lining the sides of the capsule and heaved my body into the sitting position. A secret smile hovered on my lips. Only six months ago I couldn't have even dreamed about this. But now my abs were up to the job! All thanks to Georgy, my physiotherapist, who made me give it my all at our sessions.

Using both my hands, I lifted my left leg and threw it over the edge. Now the right one. I could feel the faint tingling sensation in my calves. It was working! How cool was that?

Just think that everything had been so different only a short while ago.

THE MEMORIES of that day still came in brief flashes. A warm sunset in May. I had jumped into my Honda... I was late for a hot date. I had to take a right turn at the intersection... That stupid little boy... his ball rolled out into the road... he ran out to catch it... I yanked on the steering wheel... then darkness.

When I came round in hospital, they told me the boy was fine. His mom came to see me. She cried a lot. She thanked me.

Later, the diagnosis. The depression. Then

one day my parents met Dr. Orlov who was famous for having put much worse patents back on their feet. He told me I was in for a long struggle. If I wanted to walk again, I had to fight my own body.

It was he who suggested Mirror World's extended-immersion sessions. According to him, my brain "could use the exercise, however virtual".

My parents didn't need to be told twice. A week later, they'd already had a Glasshouse capsule installed in a dedicated room in the west wing of our house. Unexpectedly for myself, I'd gotten lost in the weirdly beautiful settings of Mirror World.

My first immersion! Even now, as I moved to my wheelchair in one strong practiced motion, I couldn't suppress a smile. It had been unforgettable. Which was more, it allowed me to move. I could walk again. I could run or dance if I wanted to!

"Reeny, your coffee's ready!" I heard Mom say again.

"Coming!" I replied, setting the wheels in motion.

THEY WERE ALL in the kitchen already. All but Dad, that is. He worked late. He always did.

Mom was busy fussing by the kitchen stove. Varya, my little sister, sat at the table with her chin on her knees, immersed in a book. That didn't stop her from periodically reaching out to sneak the nicest slices of pie from the plate without even looking.

Mickey hovered around Mom's feet, casting occasional glances at his bowl just to check if by some magic he'd been sent a second helping of his own dinner.

"Sit down before everything disappears," Mom nodded at my sister, smiling. "They eat them faster than I can make them."

"I can hear you," Varya warned, rearranging her glasses with one hand while reaching for the next slice of pie with the other. Where did it all go? The girl was as skinny as a rake!

"Your coffee," Mom placed the steaming cup onto the table and paused, looking at me with a smile.

Her gaze exuded so much love, warmth and tenderness. It was so good to be home!

"Thanks, Mom."

"Enjoy," she gave me a peck on the cheek.

"Quit fussing," Varya quipped without looking up from her book.

Smiling at her, I brought the cup to my lips. My hand was shaking. I watched Mom out of the corner of my eye: she'd noticed it too. I sighed and closed my eyes. I was in for a questioning session.

"Reeny?" Mom's voice gave, betraying her anxiety. "Is everything all right?"

Here we go.

Varya too pricked up her ears, albeit inconspicuously.

I shrugged. "Sure. Why wouldn't it be?" Still, my voice shook slightly.

"Come on, tell us," Varya said calmly, turning the page.

Mother perched herself on a chair. "Reeny, please."

They wouldn't leave me alone now, would they? "Eh... basically... how can I say it..."

"Just spit it out," Varya advised without looking up from her book. "Confession relieves guilt."

"A guy has asked me out," I said, watching their reaction.

"You mean Count?" they asked simultaneously: Varya curious, Mom smiling.

"I said no such thing!" I exploded. Had they been able to see right through me all this time?

"Yes, you did," Varya insisted, as if reading my thoughts. "You can't talk of anything else. It's always Count did this and Count did that..." she paused and added, "We might have our own Countess soon, eh, Mom?"

Ignoring Varya's quips — we'd long stopped taking her sarcasm to heart — Mom showered me with questions,

"Where is he taking you? When? What time? What are you wearing?"

"How about asking me if I'm coming first?"

"Nonsense," Varya announced. "You are not like all those soppy whiny girls, *Oh, I'm so useless and miserable! Oh, he can't possibly fall for me!* Yeah right. I bet he already knows you based your avatar on your own picture. He's probably drooling all over it."

"Picture, yes. But this," I nodded meaningfully at my legs in the wheelchair.

"This what?" Mom butted in. "You've been friends there for a long time. Nothing prevents you from staying friends in real life."

I sighed. Pointless. No good moaning about it: I was a big girl now. I was simply trying to get an unbiased view of the situation. No one in the clan knew about my problem yet. I didn't need their sympathy. Not in Mirror World.

"You know what?" I squinted one eye at them. "I think I might go."

"As if we doubted it," Varya comments, then returns to her book.

"Good," Mom says, kissing me on the forehead.

* * *

"I THINK it's here," the cab driver pulled up by a restaurant entrance.

"Thanks, Uncle Volodya," I said, rolling my wheelchair off the ramp.

Uncle Volodya had been driving me around for ages. We had his cell number so we could call him directly whenever needed. He was all right.

"You're welcome," he replied. "You sure you can manage?"

I smiled to him. "Yes, thank you. I looked this place up on the Internet. They have wheelchair access and everything."

Actually, I'd never heard of them before. The restaurant was on the opposite side of town. Normally, all of us shared lists of handicapped-friendly places: banks, pharmacists, shops, theaters and beauty salons. It was like a quest, really. I even had a map.

"Well, it's up to you," he said with a fatherly smile. "You look great, by the way. Have a nice evening. Give me a ring when you're about to leave."

"I will, thank you."

He was right. I did look good. I could see it

in men's stares as they walked past, casting me glances of surprise rather than sympathy.

I'd turned up early. Never mind. I could live with that. At least my date wouldn't witness my arrival.

So, what did we have here?

The place was called *Chez Marius*. They even had a rubber ramp. I rolled in easily.

My hands shook. My heart was about to explode. How. Utterly. Scary.

The tinted doors hissed open. Excellent. Just what I needed. These automatic doors saved you the embarrassment of pushing yourself through the doorway, especially if the door springs were tight.

The restaurant room was enveloped in safe shadows, soft music and appetizing smells.

The young hostess smiled to me. "May I have your name, please?"

"It's Irene."

She found me on her list and motioned me to follow her. "This way, please."

My wheelchair rolled softly across the floor. She walked next to me. Their staff was apparently well trained: she wasn't trying to grab at my chair to roll it herself. I might be handicapped but I wasn't helpless.

The place wasn't busy but she was taking me to a completely deserted corner. I noticed the sufficient distance between the tables. Very good. I was starting to like it here.

Still, I was shuddering. I hadn't been so scared even when we'd raided the Darkies.

The table in the darkest corner was already taken. And...

It was him. I just knew it. The evil tongues had been right, after all. His avatar was a carbon copy of himself. His skin was pallid white, though... how weird... that was the only difference.

He couldn't see me yet; he was too busy staring at the menu. His hands were shaking. No way! He was nervous too!

Finally, he looked up. His eyes were the same emerald hue.

He was looking at me.

My cheeks were burning. Thank God it was dark here.

Finally, his gaze lit up with recognition. Surprise.

I stopped. No idea why. It was probably my hands clenching the wheels.

We both froze within a few paces from each other.

Why did he look so astounded? I had every reason to be, but him?

My anxiety began to die away, replaced by cold serenity: my defense mechanism, a mask I employ against friends, including someone I used to like very much.

Coming here hadn't been such a good idea after all.

Whatever. Come what may. The sooner it was over, the sooner I'd be back home. I might do a bit of crying before bedtime, then I'd get on with my life.

I was about to roll my wheelchair forward when finally Count awoke from his stupor.

He smiled to me.

How weird. This wasn't the reaction I expected to see. Sympathy, yes. Courtesy, maybe. A fake smile, as if this was perfectly normal.

But not relief.

Count was grinning at me from the table. His gaze... I remembered it. That day, we'd been the only two left of our group. The mobs had attacked us with dogged repetition. The way he'd defended me you would have thought this was in real life. He'd been a warrior god in the flesh. We'd won. And this was the exact same look he'd given me that day. Relieved and cheerful.

So stupid of me. How could I ever have doubted him?

I hadn't expected what happened next.

His burly shoulders tensed up. You'd think it was him trying to scramble out of a wheelchair, not me. I knew this movement only too well.

Just as I squeezed my eyes tight, about to dissolve in tears, I saw the rest of him. And the edge of his wheelchair under the table.

TRANSLATED FROM RUSSIAN BY IRENE WOODHEAD
AND NEIL P. MAYHEW

THE STORY OF A RAID

A TALE FROM
THE GALACTOGON SERIES

BY VASILY MAHANENKO

"TEN DOZEN interceptors approaching from Andromeda! Distance—200 clicks."

"Multiple bogeys in the Aquarius constellation! Accelerating at 300 clicks per second! Sensors can't make them out too well, but there don't seem to be any big ships with them!"

"Our scout is reporting that the Qualians are on the move. They're looking for captains with cruisers. At the moment we're facing only bounty hunters and small-time guilds. Everyone's shocked—they didn't expect us to pull something like this."

The reports were rushing in thick and fast, mixing together and contradicting each other in a confusing torrent of information. If someone less prepared had been in the captain's place, a mere minute of this would cause panic amid the numbers and words. But Marina—captain of the level-98, A-class cruiser *Alexandria*—merely frowned and rubbed her temples. It was looking like today would be a long day...

A class-A cruiser was the pinnacle of the space fleet in the virtual universe of *Galactogon*. In terms of firepower, defense and repair capability, this vessel was second only to an orbital fortress or a Grand Arbiter (a "Judge," as the players liked to call them). At the moment, the *Alexandria* was carrying 4300 players as crew, 220 interceptors, 2 transports with 600 marines each, 10 resource harvesters, 3 resource refineries and some reserves—just in case. The *Alexandria* was an incredible threat that demanded respect and fear, and was accordingly marked for destruction by all seven of *Galactogon's* in-game Empires.

Thanks to her reputation as the "Iron Lady" as well as "a player with fortune ever on her side," Marina had never found a lack of players for her raid groups. Those who wanted to play for Kiddo, as the players called this girl of average height, were never ending. Even now, although though there were already five thousand players on the ship, there were another seven thousand waiting to take their places in real life. In the hopes that someone would drop out, encounter network problems, or pressing business IRL, they were all waiting on tenterhooks for their turn, knowing that they might never see another chance. Kiddo didn't do raids often—typically once a month—but she always came back with enormous amounts of loot which was automatically distributed among the raid party members.

"Disruptor fields to starboard. Don't let the interceptors breach it," Marina began to issue orders. "Marine brigade—be ready in five minutes. "Anton," she turned to one of the few players who had been there with her in her very first interceptor about...well, a very long time ago..."get the harvesters ready. We'll send them in behind the marines—they can begin picking up the pieces. Vanya—as soon as the bogeys are in visual range, you know what to do. Don't waste too much power."

"Roger that, Cap," a young, almost childish voice said through the intercom. Ivan was a twelve year-old, who had been discovered about two years ago and had since then become an inalienable part of the *Alexandria*. How this young man managed to operate the ship's entire fire control system on his own remained a mystery to everyone including the game developers. At a station that required up to five players on other vessels—a job that carried all kinds of problems of synchronization—Ivan simply grinned and sang. And he sang all the time, even though the kid had no sense of pitch whatsoever.

"You know, Marina," said Anton, the executive officer, chief aide, deputy and also the captain's IRL husband of five years, "if we manage to do what you have in mind, you'll have more than the seven Empires to worry about. Even the Confederate planets will deem us unwelcome. I realize that it's too late to change anything, but tell me—are you sure it's worth it? To risk everything over a humiliation you suffered such a long time ago?"

"We've already discussed this, Anton. Even if we lose right now, we'll build a second cruiser. We have the money. But getting our hands on a Legendary cruiser...besides being an upgrade across the board, it'll also...Well, you understand better than anyone. I'm ready to risk it, and every one of the five thousand players on board understands that if we go down now, we'll have to start from scratch. Launch the harvesters—I'm not about to lose this loot!"

Turning away from the screens, Marina sank into her thoughts. For now, everything was going as she had planned it—the Qualians had not anticipated an attack on one of their core planets, assuming that no one would dare mount a raid so deep in their territory. Until they managed to pull up something heavy and dangerous, her raid party had the freedom to gather resources from across several planets, and if they got lucky even plunder some depots. If those turned out to hold Raq—the game's main resource required for ship-building—then this mission would pay for itself after all...

Galactogon was a virtual game world that revolved around several core game modes:

starting from the standard "hit and run," in which a mob of players decked out in camo uniforms chased each other around with blasters—and ending in a cutting-edge space flight simulator that allowed players to conquer star systems across vast reaches of space. The game had an utterly staggering amount of players playing it—almost the entire population of Earth, the Moon, and Mars, which amounted to over ten billion people, had *Galactogon* accounts. Even if the majority only used their accounts for social media, work or education, the fact remained: Just about everyone was connected to this game.

Formally, *Galactogon* contained seven Empires, each ruled by local NPCs. Occupying provisional boundaries, the Empires were constantly waging war with one another over new territories, planets and resources—of which there were quite a multitude in the game—from the extremely expensive Raq to abundant Elo—the energy resource. In addition to the Empires, there were also a myriad of independent planets in *Galactogon*. These had allied into the Confederation, though no one took them very seriously. Players would frequently head out to these planets or their satellites in order to raid, plunder and test their recruits' command or piloting skills.

You could do whatever you wanted in this

game, from gathering resources to building robots, to repairing these robots, to commanding an enormous space ship. *Galactogon* implemented a rather curious leveling up system—experience went to level up items instead of players. A person would always remain a person; however, having in one's possession several hundred level-45, class-A interceptors would be very good for one's health. When a player's avatar died in *Galactogon*, the player was respawned on his home planet, along with all the money he had in his account. The penalty, however, was that all his items remained at the site of his death. Items, including all spaceships, were fully destructible. Destroying those left parts that could be used later, as well as the contents of the cargo holds that weren't a part of the ship. The developers had done everything possible to impress on players the main principle, which was that lone-wolves had no business playing *Galactogon.*

Everyone started out penniless on distant, remote training planets. Following a mandatory month-long tutorial and training period, players were issued a ticket to one of the seven Imperial capitals—the only thing that the game's developer ever gave to the players for free—at which point, the players were left entirely to themselves. If you wanted to be somebody in the game, you'd have to invest real money to buy clothes, equipment and even food. Nevertheless, the game also had its rejects—quite a few in fact. Each one of them thought that he would be able to make something of himself without investing any real money. You could count the amount of them that succeeded on your fingers, and Marina was certainly one of them...

"Captain, we have destroyed 72 interceptors. The others have fled. Should we pick up the wreckage?" Vanya's voice came over the general comm and the entire crew froze in place. The question of loot was being decided. According to the *Alexandria's* tradition, the captain would make the choice of whether a raid party was sent after the loot or whether the crew would have to content themselves with the experience added to their items. If they went after the loot, it'd be impossible to catch up to the fleeing interceptors. If they chased the interceptors, they could forget about the wreckage—the marauders would pick it clean. Where did they come from in this vast nothing anyway?

"Anton, send out a harvester team," the girl made her decision after a second's thought. "Attention everyone! The raid objective is to collect as much loot as possible!"

Grimacing from the eruption of joy that

instantly filled the general comm channel, Marina went on peering into the screen before her—the Qualians were taking too long by allowing her harvesters to land and begin the harvesting. It was all just too simple...

"Anton, what do the scouts say?"

"Three cruisers identified, the strongest one is a class-B at level 47, so nothing really to report at the moment. The Qualian Emperor has declared war on you and promised to send his frontline Judge after us. How long it'll take to get here is a question you can answer better than anyone else around here."

"Three hours until it reaches the central planet and another hour to us," Marina said pensively. "Attention everyone! Marines—return back to the ship. Harvesters—cease recovery operations and begin hauling the loot back. We're setting a course for Shylak XIV!"

"You've decided to double down?" Anton grinned.

"Correct," the girl replied tersely. "We have three hours to pillage all we can on the trade planet. Get ready for battle with orbital stations and a joint deployment of marines and harvesters. I couldn't care less that it's never been done before or that it's dangerous. We came here to plunder and pillage—not to twirl our thumbs out on the galactic rim."

The general comm channel fell silent. The players were afraid of saying anything for fear of drawing their captain's attention. Every man knew very well that she could replace him without even bothering to find out what his name had been. All of the responsibility for attacking Shylak—one of the Qualian trade hubs—would fall on the captain, but if the ploy fell through...No one in his right mind had even thought of attacking a trade planet on his own yet. To even attempt a breakthrough against three orbital stations was impossible. However, as far as the impossible went, the *Alexandria* was an exception...

"Cruiser *Alexandria*, you are hereby ordered to leave Imperial space immediately!" the metallic voice of the defense system blared through the intercom. "If you do not comply, you will be attacked in 20, 19, 18..."

"Anton—accelerate by 200," Marina ordered after coming to a final decision. Three class-B, level-89 orbital stations were an imposing obstacle. And yet she knew that they could be manipulated. If she would do things the way she had done repeatedly in the training simulator, then everything would work out fine. "And take control of the ship. Lisp—you're in charge of shields and disruptor fields. Marines and harvesters—launch on my mark...Three...two...one...mark!"

"Cruiser *Alexandria*! You have ignored our orders and will be terminated!"

"Vanya—fire only on my personal command!"

"I remember! Don't worry, Cap, I'll do everything to a T. Just give me the right target and I'll take care of it!"

"We've been hit!" Lisp announced from the shields station. "Full absorption! The orbital station is preparing for a full salvo!"

"Shields to bow, accelerate 300, bearing 30, turn 45 degrees."

"We've been hit! Minus ten percent durability!"

"What's with the marines?" asked the girl, ignoring Lisp's reports.

"The orbitals didn't touch them—I guess they're leaving them for the surface defense forces. Marines have entered the atmosphere and the harvesters are on approach. There're already interceptors waiting for them. We'll lose them!"

"Acceleration 700. Set bearing on a tangent with Shylak! Altitude 300 meters! It's your turn, Vanya. When you're through, I don't want to see a single interceptor within a hundred click radius!"

"I'm on it! Five seconds!"

"Twenty seconds until the orbital's full

salvo," Lisp added his two melancholy cents, but no one was paying any attention to him anymore. What Marina had planned on doing was entirely beyond the bounds of the imaginable and an attack on an already dead ship wouldn't change anything.

"Let's do it! Everyone hold on. We're about to experience true turbulence!"

"Marina, you are out of your mind," Anton injected nervously, pressing himself into his seat. "And that's what I love about you!"

A class-A space cruiser is an enormous 5-kilometer long leviathan designed to suppress enemy fleet forces in open space. Having ample maneuverability, power and defensive capability, the ship made for an excellent fleet escort and base. No one however had tried to use it like an ordinary interceptor before. The simple fear of colliding with skyscrapers kept even the pilots of these small and agile craft from descending down to 300 meters above the planet's surface. It looked like Marina had forgotten to read the instructions for piloting her ship...

"Atmospheric entry...Acceleration 700...Altitude ten thousand," the steely voice of the ship computer, which Marina refused to change on principle, reported the condition of the vessel. The crew that had remained on board the ship froze at their stations. Everyone understood that either a miracle was about take place and they would accomplish the impossible—or there'd be a flash and the planet below them would consume them in its vast embrace. "Altitude five thousand...Altitude two thousand...Collision warning! Altitude one thousand..."

Fists clenched, knuckles white, Marina peered into the screens before her. Another two seconds and...

"Altitude three hundred...Collision with Shylak XIV Parliament building! Collision with Shylak XIV Communications Ministry! Collision with..."

"Firing now!" came Ivan's joyful cry and for several seconds, the *Alexandria* turned into an enormous sun. Two hundred cannons mounted around the cruiser's circumference simultaneously came to life, blasting the planetary defense ships rising from the planet's surface.

"Altitude four hundred...Defense capability down by 40%...Adding power to shield regeneration recommended..."

"Captain, everything is clear for 120 clicks around us!" Ivan reported with satisfaction and the general comm registered the entire crew's sigh of relief—they had managed to do the impossible!

"Marines and harvesters—descend to the

planet. Commence gathering operations," added Anton and the general comm exploded with cries of celebration. Even if they were destroyed now, the harvesters would teleport the loot directly to the refineries orbiting their home planet. Regardless of how the raid went from here on, the raid party's reward was now assured.

"Five seconds until orbital salvo!" Lisp did not partake in the team's general celebration.

"Acceleration 1500, hard brake in three seconds," Marina said half to herself and the entire crew of the ship was pressed back into their seats. "Turn at 50, bearing 120..."

"You do know that a cruiser isn't meant to be used as an interceptor?" croaked Anton, but the girl wasn't listening. She had only one thing on her mind at the moment:

"Vanya—be ready to fire in ten seconds! Lisp—shields full forward!"

"Done! Orbital volley incoming!" Lisp did as ordered and reported back.

"I'm ready!" added the weapons officer with his finger hovering over a button situated apart from the rest of the controls.

"Vessel has been hit...Forty percent damage taken...Durability ten percent...Emergency repairs required immediately..."

"Let 'em have it, Vanya!" ordered the girl

over the computer's report.

"Blasting away," smirked the kid, pushing the button. "Target hit! Goddamn!"

Achievement earned: Unparalleled power! Cruiser Alexandria has reached level 100. Your ship's class has grown. Current class: Legendary. All ship parameters have increased by 20%. Durability and Energy have been fully restored.

"Scramble all interceptors to Shylak's atmosphere! Your objectives are to suppress any resistance and gather whatever loot you can!" the girl commanded over the staccato of her pulse. "First assault team—move against the capital and assist on the ground. Second assault team, stay with the harvesters. Constantine," Marina said to her head of recruiting, "I need more manpower. We'll need three hundred. Prioritize those who have harvesters or interceptors. You have ten minutes. Attention everyone—acceleration 300, turn at 240, bearing 30 degrees. Lisp—reroute shields to starboard!"

"Done!"

"Ready, Vanya?"

"You bet! A broadside really is something to behold. Did you know we'd get that much experience?"

"I had a hunch! Attack in 5, 4, 3, 2...Fire!"

New level reached: Legendary Cruiser Alexandria has reached level 101. Durability, weapons and energy have been restored by 30%.

"How much longer, Ivan?"

"Ten minutes to reload!"

"The orbital will hit us in two, then seven," Lisp immediately injected. "We might not survive the second salvo."

"We still have two harvesters in our hangers!" added Anton. "Shall we send them planetside?"

"No!" Marina snatched onto the unexpected windfall. "Send them to the wreckage of the first and second orbital station. Let them pick up the pieces!"

"Done. They're on their way! What are we going to do about the interceptors? One hundred are inbound with an ETA of five minutes."

"Get down there and storm Shylak! We have to take that depot!"

"Roger! You're a monster Marina! How did you find out about the orbitals' weakness?"

"No time to explain now. I'll tell you after the raid. What do the scouts say?"

"The capital already knows that we've taken

out two orbital stations! The Emperor has declared you a nemesis of the Empire. The Qualians have declared a temporary truce with the Precians and sent their entire fleet in our direction. They've even sent the Judge from their home world's defense garrison! Two hours until it arrives! No one's sent an armada like this against a single ship before, Marina. We've entered the pages of game lore for sure!"

"Five seconds until next orbital salvo!"

"Shields to bow, rotate thirty seconds, turn 90 degrees. What's up with the harvesters?"

"Five percent of the first station have been collected. The cruiser can be instantly repaired by 2%. It's not enough, Marina. I told you we needed to upgrade the repair system!"

"Of course, Gregory, of course! If we get out of here, I'll do more than upgrade it—I'll replace the whole thing! There'll be room now for it! But for now, wring everything you can from it. I need the ship to survive the first hit!"

"We've been hit!" declared Lisp as the cruiser shuddered. "Durability down to half. We may not survive a second hit!"

"I know! Anton, what's the situation on the ground?"

"Harvesters are operating at 100%. We've gathered forty tons of resources so far. There's no Raq in sight. The first city sector has been destroyed. The marines are picking up the loot. The depot is holding out. Their defenses are too strong. We've lost 42 interceptors. We've already gathered the wreckage and are transporting it back at the moment. And there's something else you should know..." Anton added awkwardly.

"What else?"

"One of the ships trying to flee the planet was carrying some members of the Precian race. The Precians have declared war on us too. That's two empires hunting the *Alexandria*. My congratulations!"

"Goddamn..." the girl swore under her breath, but the entire crew heard her and froze. The Iron Lady had never cursed before. Something wasn't going according to plan. "What's going on with you, Vanya?"

"Five minutes! I can't make it any earlier!"

"Lisp?"

"Durability's down to 45% We won't be able to take out the third station with a single volley! It'll take two at least! We were lucky with the first and second—but now there's no fourth station to finish off the remaining one! Our reload time is ten minutes. The orbital's is five. We won't survive three hits!"

"Vanya, when you're ready, you let me know," Marina said wearily, reclining back in her captain's chair. That was it. Nothing hinged on her anymore—she had done everything she could. From here on out, it all depended on the players themselves.

"We're hit!" the vessel shuddered again. "Durability at ten percent...We have five minutes left to live..."

"We've taken the depot!" Anton announced happily, monitoring the battle down on Shylak. "We're plundering it now! We estimate that it holds several tons of Raq. Can you imagine? Several tons! Thirty percent of the city has been destroyed. The marines are still working."

"I'm ready, Cap," Ivan reported immediately. "We can afford a salvo. Let them do the repairs later!"

"All interceptors and harvesters abandon ship! You have three minutes. How much can we repair in that time?"

"We can have her back up to thirty percent," Lisp quickly tallied up the data. "What's the point though, Marina?"

"Any player who doesn't wish to respawn must leave the ship within the next three minutes!" the girl announced into the general comm. "Thank you everyone for helping with the raid. Our loot should cover all our losses! The countdown begins now."

"I assume," said Ivan wryly, "that you will request that I stay on board?"

"Lisp, I'll need you too!"

"What would you do without me? But why don't you tell me what you have in mind?"

"What I have in mind? Nothing special. Anton, what's with the Qualians?"

"I'm staying too. The Qualian fleet will reach the central planet in an hour and reach us in another. So two hours...We don't have that time though unless you know something we don't. Well, Marina, do you?"

"I do! Ninety seconds remaining! Anyone who wants to save his equipment, abandon ship immediately!" the girl reiterated again, concealing her satisfaction. Not a single person had budged in the ninety seconds that had elapsed since her first announcement. Everyone knew that if they left her now, they'd never go on another raid with her again.

"It's time! Vanya, wait for my mark! Acceleration 2400, rotation at 20, bearing 0 degrees. Let's go!"

"No, Marina!" Anton blurted out, but his voice was lost in the deafening grating.

A dull blow shook the cruiser's hull, knocking everyone onto the floor.

"Durability at one percent," the ship's onboard computer informed the crew in its calm, steely tone. "Vessel self-destruct activating in 5, 4, 3..."

"Vanya—mark!"
"Roger that! Firing!"

New level reached: Legendary Cruiser Alexandria has reached level 102. Durability, weapons and energy have been restored by 30%.

Silence.

"The city has been 50% destroyed. The harvesters have finished scavenging the first station and are moving on to the next," Anton reported in a whisper for some reason.

"Ship Durability is at 30%. Active repairs are underway," Lisp echoed in a whisper too.

"Marina, my mom is calling me to dinner. I'll be back in fifteen minutes, okay?" said Ivan, utterly ignoring what was going on. The fact that the cruiser had just rammed an orbital station and blown it up from within did not seem to concern him one bit. Big deal—a cruiser used as a battering ram! With a commander like this, this kind of miracle is a daily occurrence.

"Okay. Attention all ship personnel—you have 90 minutes of personal time!" said the girl, shutting her eyes. "Anyone who wishes may sign out to reality or go down to Shylak and try to snatch something before the marines get their paws on it. Please mind the time. After the 90 minutes is up, the cruiser will be heading home..."

"The Qualians are rerouting everything they have in our direction," Anton reported thirty minutes later. "According to the forum chatter, they're forming a sphere around us. The Emperor has ordered them to keep us from slipping away...Marina—if we want to keep the *Alexandria* in one piece, we need to go this instant."

"I gave our men 90 minutes," replied the girl and glanced at her watch. "No one can say that I've ever gone back on my word. If we're surrounded, we'll find a weak point and break through! They'll be spread out and we'll have an easier time of it. Lisp—when will the cruiser be at full Durability?"

"We're picking up the remnants of the third station now. I estimate that we'll be able to reach 94% Durability. We don't have the materials to repair it any more than that. We can start up the Raq refineries, but we'll only manage to process 3–4% in an hour, no more. Should I start them?"

"Don't bother. Leave it as is. Anton—what's going on with the city?"

"All the defense systems have been destroyed. Some pockets of resistance remain here and there. The overall level of the interceptors has gone up by three points. The marines have gained seven. There were forty tons

241

of Raq in the depot. No more than ten percent remain now. We're making good progress in our marauding activities. This is the first time we've ever captured a planet like this and, I'm not even kidding: We've sent four million players to respawn in a mere half hour. We've never seen lucre like this!"

"New info incoming, Marina! Vrakas has decided to assist the Qualians. They have sent ten orbital stations and four Judges to complete their sphere...There'll be Grand Arbiters all around the perimeter now...It really was a good raid..."

"Cruiser *Alexandria*! You have attacked trade planet Shylak XIV of the Qualian Empire!" Forty five minutes later, the admiral in charge of the armada announced on the open channel. "We demand you surrender and pay restitution to the Empire. Otherwise, you will be destroyed and added to the Empire's blacklist. You have ten minutes to reach your decision!"

"Anton, you promised me two hours," the girl shot a teasing glance at her pale deputy. "It's only been 90 minutes and they're already here."

"Three Judges have locked on to us," Lisp reported for some reason. "What are your orders, Captain?"

"Go on with the pillaging!" smirked Marina and addressed the open channel: "This is the captain of the Cruiser *Alexandria*! Who has been authorized to accept my surrender?"

"The Imperial Counselor, currently aboard the orbital station *Nair*. Send a shuttle with no more than five people on board!"

"You may expect us in five minutes," the girl replied to the astonishment of her crew as well as the enemy admiral. The Qualian players, who had been urgently assembled from all corners of the empire to respond to the raid, couldn't believe their ears: The Iron Lady was about to surrender.

"You sure like to take risks!" Anton grinned once again. "What if it doesn't work?"

"Oh Anton," smiled the girl. "We've been together god knows how long and you still doubt me...Wait here. I'll be right back..."

✳ ✳ ✳

THE GIRL SAW a bright flash and watched the lid of the gaming capsule slowly lift up and open. Five minutes...She had only five minutes to make the phone call.

"Hi, it's me! Everything is going according to plan. The armada with the Counselor has been drawn in to Shylak...Yes, everyone...Absolutely correct... Five minutes...Okay, I'll be waiting in two minutes..."

✳ ✳ ✳

"WHAT'D I MISS?" As soon as Marina signed back into the game, Ivan's voice came over the comm. "Double damn! Where'd they dig up so many Grand Arbiters? Marina—should I reload the guns?"

"Attention raiding party," said Marina, pressing the all-comm button. "Thank you for such an entertaining seven hours! I congratulate all of you only your newly acquired loot! I am planning on conducting another raid in several months. Keep an eye on my site for further information. Those of you in interceptors, you'll have to get back on your own. Marines—I'll be waiting for you on the ship in three hours."

"Marina, I don't understand!" came Lisp's voice, while suddenly, every single player in *Galactogon* saw one and the same, game-wide notification:

The Qualian home world has been destroyed! Respawn duration: 24 hours! During this time, orbital stations and Grand Arbiters have been disabled! All Qualians: Hurry back to defend your home world from the marauders!

"You did it!" whispered Anton in awe when

the Qualian Grand Arbiters froze in place as though paralyzed.

"Lisp—send out the harvesters. With this amount of loot, we'll definitely enter the pages of history!

Pressing the all-comm button, the girl added:

"Attention all Qualian players in the vicinity! This is the captain of the Cruiser *Alexandria*! I suggest you leave this solar system before I open fire on you. You have five minutes to decide. The countdown begins now!"

The raid had been a success...

✳ ✳ ✳

TWO MINUTES BEFORE THE NOTIFICATION

"IS EVERYTHING ready?"

"Yeah. There are twenty warheads on the ship. It'll blow the capital to smithereens. Are you sure that the Judges are all gone?"

"Hold on. I have a call. It'll take a second...Okay, everything's ready. The fleet is at Shylak. We should be able to slip past the orbitals. Launch the shuttle."

"Let's do it!"

"Now let's get out of here and enjoy the

fireworks!"

❋ ❋ ❋

SIX MONTHS EARLIER

"MARINA, are you feeling all right? What do you mean, let's just destroy the Imperial Admiralty? It's not possible. There isn't a fleet in the galaxy that could even get close! A hundred orbital stations, five hundred Judges, cruisers and players with interceptors. It's unthinkable!"

"What if the capital is surrounded by nothing but orbitals? And the shuttle is stuffed chockfull of shield generators so that it can withstand several salvos from the orbitals? Would it be possible then?"

"If you cram twenty warheads into the shuttle—and by the way you still need to actually buy those—and throw in four, no, better ten shield generators and an accelerator...and if by some miracle you manage to squeeze through to their home world...then I think that yes, it might. That's *if* there won't be a Grand Arbiter in the way. They reload faster than orbitals and do much more damage too. But how are you going to manage all this?"

"Leave that to me. Your job is to find a shuttle, warheads, generators, accelerators and everything else we need. Other than that, just be within two minutes of the planet in six months. Can you do it?"

"I can. But you're insane."

✳ ✳ ✳

MANY YEARS EARLIER

"RECRUIT MARINA reporting from the Training Planet," announced the girl. "I have completed training with 100 out of 100 in all subjects. I am ready to enlist in the fleet. I wish to serve the Qualian Empire!"

"The Empire isn't interested in eager beavers who have nothing to offer," replied the fat NPC clerk without bothering to stifle his yawn. "Either purchase a starter kit or there's the door, kiddo. The Qualian navy doesn't take riffraff."

"You didn't even look me in the eyes!" objected the girl barely concealing her outrage. A month earlier, having decided to open a *Galactogon* account, she decided that she would play for the Qualians, since that Empire had the most advanced technology. However, Marina set one strict condition for herself: She would never expend a single real world penny in the game. She needed to prove that one could succeed in *Galactogon* with nothing but one's wits.

Graduating in the top of her training class, she was within her right to expect some respect, and yet...If you don't have real cash, there's the door.

"Guards! Guards!" squeaked the NPC. "Toss this garbage in the street where it belongs! The Qualian Empire isn't a charity organization!"

"Jerks..." whispered the girl. Glaring at the receding guards, she wiped the dust from her face. "We'll see which one of us is garbage!"

TRANSLATED FROM RUSSIAN BY BORIS SMIRNOV

Want to be the first to know about our latest LitRPG, sci fi and fantasy titles from your favorite authors?

Subscribe to our NEW RELEASES newsletter: http://eepurl.com/b7niIL

Thank you for reading *You're in Game!*
If you like what you've read, check out other
LitRPG novels published by Magic Dome Books.

Our latest releases:

Stay on the Wing (The Dark Herbalist Book #2)
by Michael Atamanov

NEW LitRPG Series!!
The Beginning (Dark Paladin Book #1)
by V. Mahanenko

NEW LitRPG Series!!
The Crystal Sphere (The Neuro Book #1)
by A. Livadny

Save $5.98!
By buying all three e-books of
Phantom Server LitRPG Series
by A. Livadny
or
Perimeter Defense LitRPG Series
by M. Atamanov
as a Boxed Set for $9.99 instead of $15.97!

The Way of the Shaman series by Vasily Mahanenko:
Survival Quest
The Kartoss Gambit
The Secret of the Dark Forest
The Phantom Castle

Galactogon LitRPG series by Vasily Mahanenko:
Start the Game!

Phantom Server LitRPG series by Andrei Livadny:
Edge of Reality
The Outlaw
Black Sun

Perimeter Defense LitRPGseries by Michael Atamanov:
Sector Eight
Beyond Death
New Contract

The Dark Herbalist LitRPG series by Michael Atamanov:
Video Game Plotline Tester

Mirror World LitRPG series by Alexey Osadchuk:
Project Daily Grind
The Citadel
The Way of the Outcast

The Game Master LitRPG series by A. Bobl and A. Levitsky:
The Lag

The Sublime Electricity series by Pavel Kornev
The Illustrious
The Heartless
Leopold Orso and The Case of the Bloody Tree

Moskau (a dystopian thriller)
by G. Zotov

Memoria. A Corporation of Lies (an action-packed dystopian technothriller)
by Alex Bobl

Point Apocalypse (a near-future action thriller)
by Alex Bobl

The Naked Demon (a paranormal romance)
by Sherrie L.

More books and series are coming out soon!

In order to have new books of the series translated faster, we need your help and support! Please consider leaving a review or spread the word by recommending *You're in Game!* to your friends and posting the link on social media. The more people buy the book, the sooner we'll be able to make new translations available.

Thank you!

Till next time!

www.ingramcontent.com/pod-product-compliance
Lightning Source LLC
Chambersburg PA
CBHW072215170626
46813CB00003B/943